Advertising Revolution

Advertising Revolution:

The Story of a Song, from Beatles Hit to Nike Slogan

Alan Bradshaw
& Linda Scott

Published by Repeater Books
An imprint of Watkins Media Ltd

19-21 Cecil Court
London
WC2N 4EZ
UK
www.repeaterbooks.com
A Repeater Books paperback original 2018
1

Distributed in the United States by Random House, Inc.,
New York.

Cover design: Johnny Bull
Typography and typesetting: Josse Pickard
Typefaces: Meridien / Gotham

ISBN: 9781912248216
Ebook ISBN: 9781912248223

Printed and bound in the United Kingdom

Dedicated to Harry

Contents

Introduction

*Your only motive is to make more money for your greedy selves, and in
the process you seemingly could not care less that you have trampled
and befouled the precious memories of millions and millions of people
throughout the entire world. Your kind makes me puke; you low,
vacuous, malodorous perverts.*

Consumer Letter, Mr Mileski to Nike, 1987

When Donald Trump took the podium in February 2016 to
cheering crowds, having just won the milestone first primary
election in New Hampshire, the Beatles' "Revolution" was
the song that marked his victory. How did we get to this
surreal moment, in which a song about revolution by John
Lennon—a musician whose radical left activism in the USA
was of such concern to the state that the FBI were determined
to deport him—came to be used in Trump's extraordinary
right-wing campaign?

Written in response to the May 1968 uprising in Paris, during
which streets were barricaded, factories and civic buildings
occupied, and millions of workers on strike, Lennon's message
originally prompted outrage within leftist circles and has been
listed by *National Review* as one of the great conservative rock
songs.[1] Yet in 1987, when the song that includes the lyrics, "if
you go carrying pictures of Chairman Mao, You ain't gonna
make it with anyone anyhow", featured in an advertisement

for Nike shoes, the advertisement was treated by many leftists as a betrayal of their heritage. "Revolution" is claimed by the left and right alike, and there is a long history of contestation over who has the right to identify with the song.

A parallel example is presented by Bruce Springsteen's rock anthem "Born in the USA", which was included in Ronald Reagan's presidential campaign, much to Springsteen's bemusement. As Springsteen recounts:

> "Born in the USA" remains one of my greatest and most misunderstood pieces of music. The combination of its "down" blues verses and its "up" declarative choruses, its demand for the right of a "critical" patriotic voice along with pride of birth, was too seemingly conflicting (or just a bother!) for some of its more carefree, less discerning listeners. This, my friend, is the way the pop political ball can often bounce.

As this book demonstrates, "Revolution" is a song—in fact, a series of songs—riddled with similar contradictory components and ambiguities. This is a study, then, of how a rock song can be understood in very different ways, and how that diversity of understanding becomes absorbed into political contestation: of how "the pop political ball" bounces into unexpected places. As Springsteen put it: "Records are often auditory Rorschach tests; we hear what we want to hear."[2] Arguably, the Beatles' "Revolution" and the subsequent Nike advert present us with the biggest auditory Rorschach test of all, with extraordinary consequences.

We will show that these diverse ways of understanding the song, rather than representing an obscure footnote to the song's fascinating history, were significant in marketing and consumer culture history, and constituted a decisive moment for how Nike came to be regarded as not just at the vanguard of a cultural economy of signs, but also one of the "bad apples" of corporate culture, routinely singled out for critical attention. By exploring the history of the song's ambiguity, and following this ambiguity into the Nike ad's production and cultural impact, a surprisingly rich story emerges.

The Nike campaign was credited with a dramatic turnaround in Nike sales. At the same time, it introduced the public to the ethos that would quickly transform the brand into a global giant, propelling the small Oregon agency that produced it into the stratosphere of advertising fame. While popular songs are prevalent in today's ads, the Nike ad was the first time the original recording of a rock classic was used in a major advertisement. In the world of advertising, the ad is still regarded as having pushed the boundaries of convention. As one contemporary advertiser put it, "when I saw that spot run on my parent's console TV, I knew what I wanted to do. I wanted to create ads that weren't ads."[3] Indicative of how the advertisement was understood as transcending its own genre, in 2011 the Directors Guild of America featured the Nike "Revolution" spot in its retrospective event titled "Celebration of Game Changing in Commercial Direction", wherein the event curator declared that the ad "killed jingles and stylistically captured a turning point".[4] In 2017, thirty years after the ad's release, *Rolling Stone* declared the ad as having generated a "revolution in advertising".[5]

The use of "Revolution" also provoked a furious controversy; alienated sections of Nike's potential market; resulted in the only lawsuit the Beatles ever filed against an advertiser; and, in the view of many, established Nike as the cynical multinational that soon foisted American culture upon the rest of the planet, exploited labourers in developing countries, and compelled poor children to kill for their overpriced, over-engineered shoes.

The debate that began in 1987 still rages across internet forums. For example, in a YouTube exchange, we see some excoriate Nike for using "Revolution" to sell trainers, an action seen as inconsistent with Lennon's legacy. Others emphasise the anti-revolutionary lyrics and the Beatles' own commercial exploits. One user ends the discussion by remarking that the

Nike ads still represent "a cultural event. 20 years on and people are still bitching about it!" The ambiguity regarding John Lennon's intention in relation to revolutionary politics, including his attitude towards commerce, splits the response to Nike's spot even now.

We will argue that this extreme polarisation results, above all, from reductive understandings of intentionality. One of our objectives in writing this book is to argue that if we are to understand advertising in terms of culture and politics, as we should, then we must avoid imagining a mythical monolith called "advertisers". Behind this term are brand managers, account executives, sales managers, copywriters, art directors, television producers, actors, musicians, set designers, casting chiefs, distributors, and multiple others who struggle over the competing objectives, strategies, and designs that clash, mesh, and crystallise into a final campaign. In place of what is often a dense thicket of personal, political, economic, and aesthetic ends, it is simply too reductive to assume that advertising exists for a single goal: to sell stuff. We want to present a history of an advertisement that takes into account the collective work of diverse participants, each of whom brings an often deeply different intention. Our argument is that assessing these intentions, either real or inferred, is central to the formation of the public response.

We revisit advertising in a way that insists upon its aesthetic nature and its collaborative structure, as a genre that should be understood using concepts from the arts as well as the sciences. Rather than accept that an advertisement's meaning will be precisely determined and encoded during its production, and then decoded by the public in a way that can be accurately predicted, this story explores the unpredictability of what happens when advertising texts containing unstable cultural content are released into the "social fabric".[6] By exploring the unpredictability of the public response and the often arbitrary process of production, a way of thinking about advertising emerges that is very different from landmark critical analyses by authors like Judith Williamson and Jean Kilbourne, who seem to imagine advertisements as finished and stable texts whose singular meaning can be declaratively analysed, and advertising production as a perfected science always capable of creating the desired result. This is a story, in other words, of texts that get out of control.

Within anthropological studies of commodities, there is a tradition in which scholars "follow the thing",[7] that is, trace the production and movement of a commodity: from the cultivation of its raw materials right through to its manufacture, distribution, consumption, and eventual disposal. Here we attempt an equivalent venture: to track the life-course of an advertisement and to follow its biographical trajectory. The core questions become: What are the key components of the ad? Who are the central figures? What are the key moments? How are pivotal transactions managed? What apparently tangential issues divert, recast, and redirect the initial project? Throughout, how is the advertisement and its content transformed – and how does it transform itself – from stage to stage, context to context?[8]

Proceeding in this way allows us, we believe, to develop a much broader appreciation of advertising as a major force of cultural politics and, we hope, to tell a fascinating story along the way.

Chapter One
Intentionality

By definition, advertising frames messages with attributions of an intention to sell. Before turning to the song and the advertisement, we want to address what this notion of "intention" really means, how it can be applied to cultural criticism, and why we believe it is an important concept for understanding advertisements and their cultural effects.

We argue that the way we perceive intentions forms the basis for diverse understandings of the Beatles' song and of the subsequent advertisement. Those who shared the belief that commercial intent de-sacralised John Lennon's political intentions developed an oppositional interpretation. Indeed, the interpretations for both the Beatles' song and the Nike spots aligned according to broader beliefs regarding the appropriate relationship between commercial speech, artistic expression, and political action.

From this starting point, the use of celebrities in advertising is no simple matter of a direct transfer of meaning from celebrity to brand. This is to say that it is too simple to treat celebrities like manageable commodities ("human brands"), because they are real people with their own problems and politics. Therefore, references to celebrities in advertisements will be interpreted through the lens of their lives or work, and forcefully framed by the ad's own apparent intention. The mercurial being who was John Lennon proved to be as unmanageable in death as he was in life; the events of his actual life were brought to bear in the public response to the advertisement, and this endorsement event was, for some consumers and press, a negative event for Nike.

The "Revolution" story thus leads us further into popular music's cultural situatedness by showing its fluid political and cultural status – sometimes sacred, sometimes profane, sometimes art, other times commerce – and therefore pulls us into the problematic and dynamic way in which standards of "authenticity" become invoked. Our main objective, however, is to introduce intentionality into our understanding of advertising. A handful of marketing studies[1] have already documented different rhetorical strategies that define the relationship between advertising agencies and their clients, or the companies that hire them. These are manifest in divergent creative philosophies, varying concepts of consumption, and different preferences in campaign measurement. However, when studies are designed to measure effects on consumers, this heterogeneity of inputs goes unrecognised. So, when Demetrios Vakratsas and Tim Ambler published their ambitious review, "How Advertising Works: What Do We Really Know?" in the *Journal of Marketing*,[2] they followed a longstanding practice in advertising research: they characterised the producers of advertising in one word – "advertisers". Further, they assumed this actor to have the same oversimplified objective as that consistently inferred by the studies they canvassed: "advertisers" want sales. This is the casual convention that prevails.

As we will show, critics of advertising often draw from a tradition in which intention is excised, often in order to affix blame for major social ills. Thus, advertising scholars in business, media, and cultural analysis often draw conclusions, and even assign culpability, based on tacit but unsubtle assumptions about what advertisers intend. From this perspective, a sort of conspiracy theory discourse arises in which we are led to imagine that advertisers and marketers deliberately encode commodities with racism and misogyny because they have malevolent intentions. It is not a matter of being an apologist for the advertising sector to say that there must be a better way of understanding advertising as a matter of cultural politics. It is with reference to this problem that we turn toward theories of intentionality.

The intention of a commercial campaign – its objectives, strategies, and purposive design – is an important condition of its construction. The intention to increase sales is often at odds with the intention to build the brand, although both are overriding goals of most marketing enterprises and ad campaigns. Commercials are usually produced through a collaboration between a client, who makes money by making things, and an advertising agency, who makes money by making messages. Ad agencies, though they often pretend their first concern is client sales, are never remunerated as a percentage of the volume of sales. Instead, their hopes for prosperity lie in making messages good enough to win increased budgets, additional projects, and new clients. So the two partners are often working toward different, if related, ends, in addition to being inspired by different assessments of the market situation, profiles of the target consumer, theories of "how advertising works", and aesthetics around how ads should look and sound. Further, the advertising industry has long entertained competing philosophies, each of which can lay claim to its great campaigns and famous proponents. Add to this the professional roles played by the makers involved (the producers of graphics, copy, sound, film) as well as the personal agendas that all humans bring to a task (impressing competitors, looking to cover one's backside) and one can easily understand why advertising leader Marion Harper likened the painting of a whirling cockfight that hung in his office to "the history of the advertising business".[3]

Simply outlining the potential complexity involved in advertising intentions suggests how elaborate theories of intentionality must be. Indeed, the concept of intention has been the subject of intense focus in rhetoric, hermeneutics, philosophy, law, and the arts during the latter half of the twentieth century. Nearly all of this work takes a single essay as the point of departure: W.K. Wimsatt and Monroe Beardsley's "The Intentional Fallacy", from their 1954 book, *The Verbal Icon*.[4] Written during a paradigm shift away from a school of literary theory concerned with intention and effect, this essay was a seminal text of the "New Criticism" movement, which tried to rival science in objectivity by cutting both intention and effect out of criticism's analytical scope (along with history and cultural context) and focusing on the text alone. The New Critics sought to base their judgement of what was or was not art strictly on the presence or absence of certain formal features. Though the New Critics' gatekeeping ambitions may seem antique, similar judgments about what counts as art figured heavily in the reception of "Revolution" in both its Beatles and Nike versions. Interestingly, allusion and paradox (or irony) were the features New Critics valued most, devices both central to evaluating the Beatles' oeuvre and the Nike ad.

The New Criticism was supplanted by a crush of other theories – among others, structuralism, feminism, and Marxism. Many of these were also axiomatically unconcerned with intentionality, but two schools in ascendance in the 1970s, rhetoric and hermeneutics, focused on rehabilitating intention in order to check a trend toward esoteric interpretations. Hermeneutic scholar E.D. Hirsch decried the fashionable rush toward extreme polysemy, a "willful arbitrariness and extravagance in academic criticism" in which "a theory was erected under which the meaning of the text was equated with everything it could plausibly be taken to mean".[5]

The elimination of intent from studies of literature was followed in fields that analysed other artistic and popular forms. For instance, Judith Williamson's 1978 *Decoding Advertisements* set the pattern for a large body of advertising criticism that followed:

Advertising seems to have a life of its own; it exists in and out of other media, and speaks to us in a language we can recognise but a voice we can never identify. This is because advertising has no "subject." Obviously people invent and produce adverts, but apart from the fact that they are unknown and faceless, the ad in any case does not claim to speak from them, it is not their speech. Thus there is a space, a gap left where the speaker should be; and one of the peculiar features of advertising is that we are drawn in to fill that gap, so that we become both listener and speaker, subject and object.[6]

Williamson executed, in this brief passage, the same finesse condemned by other critics, from E.D. Hirsch to David Bordwell,[7] whereby she inserts herself in place of both author and reader. From this position, Williamson proceeded, unencumbered by the need to provide evidence of either intent or effect, to construct a theoretical field around hundreds of ads chosen according to no clear scheme and for which she provided little by way of historical, cultural, or competitive context.

The point is not to dispute that there is ideological content in advertisements, nor to reject Williamson's well-stated concerns, around issues of gender representation in particular. Rather, our concern is one of method. To insist that a singular and stable reading of advertisements can be produced on the basis of a structural analysis that does not consider any actual reader response, nor any authorial intention, nor any specificities of the process of production (apparently Williamson sees the production of all advertisements as following the same general ideological conventions), must inevitably lead to flawed conclusions and even, we argue, an overstatement of advertisements' reach and capability. Even if it is true that ideology is encoded in advertisements (a point that we do not contend), we cannot assume that this ideology will always function, that there was a specific and deliberate encoding by the advertisement producers, or that there will ever be identifiable moments of audience decoding in the way that the cultural critic anticipates.

Further, the forms of ideology encoded in ads as explained by Williamson are deeply complex and require a sophisticated understanding of notoriously difficult theorists, like Jacques Lacan, to interpret. Apparently, we are to take it that advertisers somehow tacitly know how to encode such complex ideology in each advertisement, as though all are experts in applying Lacanian psychoanalysis. Considered as a generalisation for an entire profession, this is surely unlikely. Put differently, as marketing faculty who are familiar with the mainstream textbooks that teach advertising to the sector, we can confirm that there is very little overlap in terms of how the critical theorists believe advertising works and how advertisers themselves account for the products of their labour. An interesting counterpoint is the argument that ideology comes embedded in the reproduction of practices, and therefore its presence in a text is not at all contingent on the active awareness of the author (as per the culture industry thesis of Adorno and Horkheimer). Our point in this book, however, is simply to suggest that a more easily defended explanation for the cultural politics of this particular advertisement may be provided by returning to theories of intentionality.

In any case, by the end of the 1980s, this interpretive tactic of structural analysis had become *de rigueur* in advertising criticism (though it was increasingly challenged in other fields). Furthermore, a concrete intentionality on the part of the advertising critic was often assumed. For instance, in his 1987 *The Codes of Advertising*, Sut Jhally moves – within the space of a page or two – from asserting the invisibility of the author of advertisements to the following suggestion:

Consider how consumers would react if the following kinds of meaning were associated with particular commodities: that a product was produced by child labour in a Third World dictatorship; that raw materials were mined by young children;

that a product was produced by someone working eighteen hours a day for subsistence wages in nations such as Korea or Taiwan; that making a product used up scarce non-renewable resources or destroyed traditional ways of life for whole peoples (as in the Amazon region); or that a product was produced by scab labour. All these things, I believe, would severely impact on the meanings of consumption, on the *way* we buy.[8]

This body of criticism, like the texts it analysed, was distinguished by a notion of firm intentions regarding intervention in the concrete world. Jhally's book appeared the same year as Nike's "Revolution" campaign; within two years, there were substantive attacks on Nike for labour abuses just like those Jhally had detailed.

Another highly influential advertising critic of this era was Jean Kilbourne, whose series of videos, entitled "Killing Us Softly", preceded the Nike "Revolution" ad and, like Jhally, primed cultural commentators for a critical response. Like Williamson, Kilbourne's work was influential in developing feminist critiques of advertising and raising awareness of how advertising misrepresents and objectifies women's bodies. Kilbourne directly implicates advertisers in general societal problems like violence against women and eating disorders. Thus framed, advertising is a serious matter of public health and conduct; ads are "killing us softly". As for Williamson, the problem is a methodological one. Kilbourne's method similarly presents advertisers in monolithic terms and the entire sector is presumed to operate according to the same insidious and malicious principles. Direct causal relationships are declared to exist between advertising and societal ills. Clearly, causal relationships can be extremely difficult—often impossible—to prove, and this shouldn't prohibit critical theorists from engaging in speculative thought. The issue, however, is that Kilbourne's mode of analysis is based on both highly speculative analysis and little concern with the actual process of advertising production and reception. Critical analysis, we suggest, is hardly best served by a popular analytic culture reliant on speculation and disregard for the actual producers and consumers of the phenomenon in question.

What complicates the matter further is that there may well be a heuristic relationship between the influence of critical analysis of advertisements and the public and media response to advertisements. We believe that the discourse of criticism that grew up around advertising between the late 1970s and the late 1980s had an impact on the fate of Nike as a brand, one that was propelled in part by a reaction against the use of "Revolution".

We propose a shift in interpretive practice advocated by other critics of mass culture, including David Bordwell, E.D. Hirsch, Michael Baxandall and others in the "fine arts", that involves reinserting intention as a crucial interpretive anchor on one side of a two-way discourse between maker and audience. Such an approach is not unlike that advocated by Stuart Hall who, for example, emphasised that text construction is an active social, cultural, and political affair consisting of social interaction between different practices.[9] This dialogic model allows for readings that may fit the author's intention, but in which increasingly sophisticated and vocal consumers can also resist this intent, and thus arrive at readings that are negotiated or, indeed, oppositional. From such a perspective, it would be entirely erroneous to understand the intentions that drove the mode of production as the prime determinant of how the text is ultimately "encoded" with particular meanings. Hence, cultural studies, as advanced by Hall, becomes the study of practices and processes whose interactions generate contingent outcomes that cannot always be anticipated during production, and it is the relationality of these non-reducible practices that should form the basis of analysis. This form of cultural studies analysis, we suggest, coheres with the approach of emphasising intentionality.

Attending to the circumstances of intention will also allow us to reframe the discourse of advertising as a community of practice in which the makers see themselves engaged in a creative craft, as well as a commercial endeavour, and thus consciously maintain links with other "art worlds", such as music and film. As we shall see, such reframing is crucial to understanding the advertisers' actions in the Nike case. Intentionality thus helps us to open out into the larger cultural discourse, while grounding the processes through which individual messages are produced and disseminated, and the way they affect consumer response. This approach has been called "historical poetics".[10]

Theorists in other fields tease out aspects of artistic intentionality for which there are already terms in advertising practice. They separate the desired outcome from the plan for attaining it, and distinguish the goal and the plan from the selection of elements that appear in the final message; yet they group all of these under the umbrella of "intention". In advertising terms, then, these theorists would separate the sales and marketing goals, the marketing and advertising strategies, and the choice of executional features–but would consider them all part of the overarching intention, largely because each points to, implies, and informs the other.

We should be concerned with intention because what a reader thinks the speaker is trying to accomplish in a particular message forms the foundation of the meaning they gain from it and, therefore, their reaction. This is particularly true when the text signifies obliquely, whether through reference to a previous text (allusion) or through forms that purposefully dissemble (irony, satire). Evidence establishing authorial intent is, therefore, a central concern. However, some authors have ambivalent intentions, some lie about their intention, change their mind about the text, revise it, alter their position relative to it, or simply misremember the circumstances, thus creating a contradiction in the available evidence–and a loophole through which multiple readings can claim validity. As we'll see, it was such authorial vacillation that provided permission for readers to claim radically contradictory readings of "Revolution".

The need for such "permission" arises because readers often serve their own motives by making competing claims for the meaning of a text. As argued by Hirsch, the act of reading is itself intentional: "Any normative concept of interpretation implies a choice that is required not by the nature of written texts but rather by the goal that the interpreter sets himself." The rush to claim superior legitimacy for an interpretation is often inseparable from the means of attaining social or political ascendance – the challenge is to find a normative principle with which to buttress the case, and, as Hirsch puts it, "the only compelling normative principle that has ever been brought forward is the old-fashioned ideal of rightly understanding what the author meant."[11] The intention to read "Revolution" as a revolutionary anthem and the intention to read Nike advertising as a reactionary text of co-optation both feature prominently in our story as it unfolds; in the process, Lennon's authorial intention becomes a political football.

Other forms of intention are also germane. The institutions through which art is distributed tend to hark back to past practices and previous texts in the same genre, inhibiting innovation. Thus, the institutions involved act as a kind of counter-intentional force in the creation of the text. Since advertising is a collaborative form, one must also contend with multiple authors, who are often responding to different institutions and agendas. In the various forms of Lennon's "Revolution", we will look to the influences of his collaborators, most notably Paul McCartney and Yoko Ono, for an explanation of the song's genesis. Once you take into account the influence of collaborators and editors or impresarios on the intent of a text, you necessarily open the door to multiple versions, each of which might lay claim to being the definitive one. The direction of the revisions is itself an indication of intent – and should therefore be traced in a teleological manner. The direction of intent would be important for any advertising campaign because individual ads usually stand in intentional relationship to other ads in the same campaign or to other campaigns for the same product.

Advertising as a genre strives toward novelty (the constant drive to "break through the clutter") and often shows marked shifts across campaigns that reveal the aesthetics and concerns of a given time. For instance, Roland Marchand notes the shift in the look of print ads as America moved from the Jazz Age to the Depression.[12] Shifts across the pop music genre (in 1968) and advertising (in 1987) mark our story here. Art historian Michael Baxandall introduced the term "*troc*" to explain these large-scale discursive shifts:

> [*Troc*] is a model of a relation in which two groups of people are free to make choices, which interact on each other. Typically it involves a degree of competition among both producers and consumers, between whom it is a medium of non-verbal communication: parties on either side can make statements with their feet, as it were, by participating or abstaining … a choice on any one side has consequences for the range of choice on both sides.[13]

The *troc* (which roughly translates from French as "swap"), though constrained by genre conventions and institutions, is a fundamentally forward-looking phenomenon: "One assumes purposefulness – or intent or, as it were, 'intentiveness' – in the historical actor but even more in the historical objects themselves. Intentionality in this sense is taken to be characteristic of both. Intention is the forward-leaning look of things." Thus, the *troc*'s intention "speaks to the will to innovate, to break free of past patterns, and describes the movement toward the future of the genre".[14] The *troc*'s outer border is also important to mark: the edge of what readers can anticipate and comprehend is the "horizon of expectations".[15] Here we find the limits to what a producer can do without confusing the audience – or offending it. Both the "Revolution" song and the Nike ad pushed hard against the horizon of expectation – some would say pushed past it – with attendant consequences.

In theories of intention, the relationship between the impact of the text and any person, group, or situation is its "significance". Here, however, we will use "significance" narrowly to refer to the impact of the text on the future choices for its *troc*. The effect a watershed campaign like Nike has on future ad campaigns is only one compelling reason we offer for the importance of understanding how such campaigns come into being.

In the narrative that follows, we trace intentions behind both song and commercial, then relate them to the bifurcated reader responses that ultimately led to the powerful, yet oddly paradoxical, brand we know as Nike. To prepare this commentary, we began at the National Museum of American History's Modern Advertising Archives, a unit of the Smithsonian Institution. The Nike collection there includes audiotapes of interviews with players involved in its advertising from its beginnings in the 1970s through the 1980s. It also includes all the commercials produced for Nike during that period, some marketing research, and a smattering of correspondence and legal documents, particularly those surrounding the rights to use "Revolution".

In addition to the Smithsonian archives, we used public resources documenting the Beatles and their work, as well as the social response to both the music and the advertising. Specifically, we ran an analysis of all the materials covered by the *Readers' Guide to Periodical Literature* in the United States and retrieved all printed work listed under topics like "John Lennon" or "Nike". In England, we scoured the British Library's microfilms of both music trade magazines and the international radical press for commentary on Lennon and "Revolution" at the time that *The White Album* was made. We believe we have made use of all the available published sources on Nike, the Beatles, and John Lennon, including company histories like *Swoosh*,[16] critical analyses like *Nike Culture*,[17] biographies like *Come Together*,[18] and films like *The U.S. vs John Lennon*.[19] Finally, we have lovingly listened to "Revolution" and *The White Album* many times.

Considering intentionality across its various levels and complexities allows us to think about and understand both the production and reception of advertisements in ways that contrast with conventional critical approaches. For us, to consider intentionality is to properly regard the cultural and political context in which texts appear and are encountered. From this starting point, it is important to note that the cultural and political context from which the song "Revolution" emerged was extraordinarily intense. It is to that story that we now direct our attention.

Chapter Two
The Song

In 1968, just before John Lennon wrote "Revolution", Martin Luther King was assassinated. That same year, student radicals had been forcibly removed from Columbia University's administration building in New York by police; the brutal Prague Spring had continued in Czechoslovakia; violence had erupted between protesters and police in London's Grosvenor Square; and students and trade unionists had joined forces in their millions in Paris, bringing the state to the verge of collapse. The Cultural Revolution was underway in China, led by the Red Guard youth corps, and in Vietnam millions were being slaughtered. During the summer, as Paul McCartney and John Lennon argued over the musical style of "Revolution", a massacre preceded the Olympic Games in Mexico City, Robert Kennedy was assassinated, and European student radical Rudi Dutschke was shot. But when "Revolution" was composed, the Beatles were far from this upheaval–reeling in the traumatic aftermath of the suicide of their manager Brian Epstein, they took off to India to meditate with the Maharishi in Rishikesh.

Remote from the world they were escaping, John decided to address the historical moment by penning "Revolution", a song that explicitly engaged with the politics of the day. John had, in March 1966, inadvertently stumbled into deep controversy when he told a London journalist that he regarded the Beatles as "more popular than Jesus". While the comment attracted little notice in the UK, in the USA it generated enormous resentment, especially in the South, where some radio stations banned the Beatles and anti-Beatles protests were held. Brian Epstein seriously considered cancelling the Beatles' US tour and arranged press conferences to quell the storm. By the time of their concert in Memphis in August 1966, a highly contentious affair that went ahead despite death threats, a firecracker set off on stage caused the Beatles to fear that they were being fired upon. In this context, the Beatles refrained from further political commentary and controversial statements, and this remained the policy until Epstein's suicide in 1967. By 1968, John was intent on being directly political. As he explained two years later:

> I wanted to put out what I felt about revolution, I thought it was time we fuckin' spoke about it, the same as I thought it was about time we stopped not answering about the Vietnamese war, on tour with Brian. We had to tell him, "We're going to talk about the war this time, we're not going to just waffle." And I wanted to say what I thought about revolution. I'd been thinking about it up in the hills in India. And I still had this "God will save us" feeling about it. "It's going to be all right." … But that's why I did it, I wanted to say my piece about revolution. I wanted to tell *you* or whoever listens and communicate, to say "What do you say? This is what I say."[1]

At the time, folk artists like Joan Baez and Bob Dylan were strumming political anthems for the anguished young. However, at our story's opening, rock music was viewed as trivial, inartistic, and apolitical – a purely commercial response to the fantasies of adolescent libido.

But while the Beatles had yet to explicitly address politics in their music, they were nonetheless undergoing a radical transformation. From 1963 to 1966, the Beatles had changed from being "nothing but a good rock 'n' roll band singing unremarkable romantic jingles in an extra-loud and somewhat raucous style" to a "sophisticated and highly talented group of composer-lyricist-performers who could seriously be considered among the foremost artists of their time"; they had changed from a "group of mopheads in suits" to "long-haired bohemians in psychedelic dress".[2] This transformation was evident in their music too. For example, while the prior period was defined by popular romantic songs grounded in simple boy-girl relationships, from 1965 onwards they started to evangelise for a specific type of romanticist philosophy. The songs "The Word", "Strawberry Fields Forever", "Fool on the Hill", "Nowhere Man", "Glass Onion", and "Within Without You" can be interpreted as the Beatles offering their listeners a guide to a truer vision of the world, which, while perhaps not recognised as conventionally or explicitly political, at least in the conventional sense, was nonetheless clearly intended as an intervention into how people lived their lives.[3]

The Troc

Hard as it is to imagine a time when rock was not considered political, the music trade press of 1968 shows unmistakable evidence of this state of affairs. "What is the role of the pop group in 1968? Has it become a valued contributor to the arts? Or does it remain a sordid outlet for musical incompetence designed solely to reap vast profits? The latter concept is the one still held by the public at large," wrote Chris Welch, a British pop critic, in August. He continued:

> The curious situation that now obtains is that creative, thinking young musicians have taken the initial concept of the pop group and goaded it forward ... They have maintained the same instrumentation, appearance and business approach, work towards hit singles and mass appreciation, yet their music and attitudes are far in advance of the early days of the sound still affectionately called "rock and roll" in America, and simply "pop" here.[4]

The debate considered whether rock was becoming serious artistically and politically engaged: articles with titles like "Don't laugh, but the next step could be pop as political power" appeared.[5] Jefferson Airplane, the Doors, Country Joe and the Fish were held up as exemplars of a new breed of "Underground" groups. The identifiable marks included more varied and inventive music, more poetic lyrics, longer songs, and political commentary.[6]

Many, including artists themselves, evaded the notion that pop could be either artistically serious or politically engaged. The Rolling Stones, for example, released "Street-Fighting Man" during summer 1968, and the song was promptly banned from some US radio stations for encouraging violence. Yet Mick Jagger, in a trade press interview,[7] pointedly ridiculed the notion that the song was political. Similarly, Paul McCartney, interviewed after the release of "Revolution", insisted that, "in the end, it is always only a song".[8] Even so, it is clear that, from the radical underground to Fleet Street, the media were pressuring the Beatles to engage with the issues of the day, leading some to defend the group who, "after all, however rich they are, are really only a musical group and not the conscience of the nation."[9] By October, competing camps had emerged: "on one side, the traditional-styled pop entertainers and, on the other, the progressives who believe that it can be a more permanent thing, that their music can be both Art, with a capital A, and meaningful."[10] By the time *The White Album* appeared, even consumer letters sent to the press discussed the new schism.[11]

The Product

When they returned to London and set about recording "Revolution", John sang lying down in order to convey a meditation-like serenity for the slow-tempo, bluesy song. Dispute arose between the musicians, with Paul, Ringo, and George deeming the song to be too slow and insufficiently commercial, while John insisted that the slow tempo allowed the lyrics to be more clearly understood by listeners, as befitted the song as a political statement. John gave way, and a subsequent hard-rock and fast alternative arrangement was quickly conjured and recorded.

It was the faster, latter recording that first appeared as the flipside to "Hey Jude" at the end of August, just as televisions stations were broadcasting the Chicago police battering protesters at the Democrat Conference. The single, "Hey Jude/Revolution", appeared during this sharp artistic and political shift. Both cuts on the new record were edgy in an "underground" sort of way: "Hey Jude" was more than seven minutes long, hard-rocking "Revolution" was political, and both were lyrically well beyond the romance-oriented doggerel that had prevailed in pop. When it was released on August 30, the single rocketed to the top of the charts in the UK and the US. In the glow of this success, the Beatles' press manager announced a new album would debut in time "to catch the pre-Christmas sales rush".[12]

The Beatles, with its slower "Revolution 1", was indeed released on November 22 and went straight to the top of LP charts on both sides of the Atlantic—even though its high price (due partly to being a double album and partly to a luxury tax slapped on it by the British government) put it "beyond the reach of all but the idle rich".[13] The record quickly became known as *The White Album* because it appeared in a plain white sleeve, with the title only die-stamped on the cover. Richard Hamilton, "the inventor of British pop art", designed it explicitly to look like one of "the most esoteric art publications ... To further this ambiguity, I took it more into the little press field by individually numbering each cover".[14] The numbering was intended by both Hamilton and the Beatles as a joke—making a "limited edition" out of what was to be a massive first run of production. *The White Album*, therefore, was informed by an irony that played commerce against art; like Pop Art, the album took an ambiguous stance toward both.

More irony, as well as allusion, saturated the music. Like *Sgt. Pepper* before it, *The White Album* differed from other pop music in the way it quoted musical styles from other times and places – it is pastiche *par excellence*. *The White Album*'s songs range widely in emotional content, however. Indeed, a word like "irony" is not sufficiently calibrated to capture the array of stances taken; instead, words like "satire", "parody", and "spoof" – even "lament" – are needed in addition. The songs were also full of strange narratives that had nothing to do with romance. One song, "Glass Onion", was a direct challenge to listeners not to read too much into the Beatles' music,[15] but, appearing as it did among so many songs that stretched the limits of conventional understanding, it is rather an empty gesture.

The Texts

There are three versions of "Revolution". The soft, "shoo be doo wop" version, called "Revolution 1", was recorded first, though it appeared on *The White Album* three months later than the hard-rock single. The song is written in the format of an imagined dialogue between John Lennon and a revolutionary. It is a dialogue in which the proselytiser, however, is silent and we hear instead Lennon's various sceptical rebuttals. Each verse begins with two refrains of limited agreement from John – "You say you want a revolution", which continues with "Well, you know, we all want to change the world". This pattern persists through various iterations: "You say you've got a real solution" earns the response, "Well, you know, we'd all love to see the plan"; and "You tell me that it's evolution" is followed by, "Well, you know, we all want to change the world". Interestingly, perhaps reflecting John's millionaire status, one refrain goes: "You ask me for a contribution / Well, you know, we're all doing what we can". In the third refrain of each verse, John articulates his critical distance, "But when you talk about destruction, don't you know that you can count me out", and "But if you want money for people with minds that hate / All I can tell you is, brother, you'll have to wait" and "But if you go carrying pictures of Chairman Mao / You ain't gonna make it with anyone anyhow". The chorus consists of three repetitions of the line "Don't you know it's gonna be all right".

Though it does not appear in the hard-rock version, Lennon adds the word "in" to the end of the sixth line, so the line comes out "Don't you know that you can count me out (in)." We have put the additional word in parentheses to reflect the way it is sung–out of grammatical and musical syntax–and because the word does not appear in the printed lyrics of the sleeve to *The White Album*. At no point in either version does Lennon sing, "Count me in", though some subsequent accounts, including his own in *Rolling Stone* two years later, say that he does.[16] The reassurance throughout that "it's gonna be all right" is not exactly a call to arms; this refrain is punctuated by the "shoo be doo wops" in the background. In the hard-rock version, the full refrain is not repeated and there are no "doo wops"; instead, the words "all right" are sung, or rather howled, up to eight times.

But for the "(in)", the lyrics are a solid condemnation of revolution as a political strategy. One might even take the song to reject change in the form of "evolution", a "real solution" or "the plan", even in the form of changed constitutions or institutions, in favour of the directive to "change your head" or "free your mind instead".

The softer "Revolution 1", with its seemingly sarcastic stance and smug "shoo be doo wops" is the hardest to hear as a radical anthem. Perhaps this is why most of those who later claimed "Revolution" as a protest song refer to the hard-rock style of the single version, even when claiming the words, "Count me in", which are suggested (but not actually sung) only in the soft, *White Album* version. The single, with its aggressive rhythm, raw voice, and occasional howls, sounds angry. The distortions in the guitar suggest an amp on the verge on being blown by too much stress, perhaps evocative of violence. It is by far the most distorted of all Beatles songs, as the producer George Martin recalled: "We got into distortion on that, which we had a lot of complaints from the technical people about. But that was the idea: it was John's song and the idea was to push it right to the limit. Well, we went to the limit and beyond".[17] The distorted effect was generated by plugging the guitars directly into the mixing desks and allowing the needles to go straight to red. Not only did this radical act shock the sound engineers, who believed that avoiding distortion was one of their most basic professional functions, but the distortion effect – today very common in hard rock – would have sounded extremely harsh and very unusual to the average listener of the day. Still, the words have no mitigating "(in)" – and, since this was the second version, it suggests that the teleology of the intention was toward "count me out".

"Revolution No. 9" seems to bear little resemblance to the other versions; however, it is, in fact, a palimpsest, in which "Revolution 1" was overlaid with a scramble of electronic sounds and nonsensical phrases ("Take this brother, may it serve you well." "The Twist, the Watusi." "Hold that line, block that kick."). The phrase "number nine", sounding like an old radio test, is repeated throughout. Biographers have remarked that the number nine had private significance to Lennon (it was his birthdate and so on). John himself, however, told the press that the sounds of "Revolution No. 9" were meant to mimic what actual revolution would sound like – chaotic, discordant, violent.[18] So, again, looking at this as a set of texts in a teleological relationship, the intention seems to move against revolution, rather than toward it.

There were, however, two less public and less easily retrievable versions. One was the initial demo that Lennon had recorded to show the song to the other Beatles. This recording was made before the lyrics were even complete; it says only "count me out". However, a promotional video recorded and aired before the release of The White Album (accessible on YouTube), is a mix of the "Revolution 1" and "Revolution" styles, in which Lennon sings "count me out (in)", but the doo-wops are still there.[19] Notably, the director of the promotional video, Michael Lindsay-Hogg, recalled only one specific demand from John:

"Whatever else you do in the song, I think I ought to have a close-up on the line "if you go carrying pictures of Chairman Mao, you ain't gonna make it with anyone anyhow", because *That* is the lyric in the song."[20]

By inserting these texts into the teleology of the song, we get an intention that moves back and forth between "out" and "in", although the overall message remains pretty anti-revolution. John Lennon's explanation for the "in/out" movement is suitably ambivalent:

> On one version I said "Count me in" about violence, in or out, because I wasn't sure. But the version we put out said "Count me out," because I don't fancy a violent revolution happening all over. I don't want to die; but I begin to think what else can happen, you know, it seems inevitable.[21]

The authors of the concordance to the Beatles' songs, Colin Campbell and Allan Murphy, claim that the addition of the word "in" was important enough as to "significantly modify the overall sentiment expressed in the song", and, interestingly, they interpret the ambiguity as marking the Beatles' "deep concern for honesty (which) forces them into the ironic mode for only in this way can the essential ambiguity of truth be captured". Campbell and Murphy therefore place Revolution's "in/out" movement within a broader tendency found in Beatles' songs to record oppositions and tensions; for example, they relate the "in/out" movement of "Revolution" with how "pools of sorrow" appear alongside "waves of joy" in "Across the Universe", or how in other songs hello is turned into goodbye, day into night, man into woman, joke into hymn, and the solemn into a joke.[22]

The Band

It is incontestable that the Beatles were a highly commercial group; as John Lennon said during the Sixties: "What's wrong with commercialisation? We're the most commercial band on earth!"[23] This commercial intent was most evident that summer in the founding of Apple Corps, a tax dodge prompted by the suicide of Brian Epstein, in which the Beatles sought to take control of their own business and, perhaps, to raise a business empire. They created a conglomerate out of thin air, a paper organisation that had multiple subsidiaries–Apple Music, Apple Retail, Apple Films, Apple Electronics, Apple Records–"that appeared all at once like a conjuring trick at the imperious clap of four multimillionaire's hands".[24] But this multinational corporation was also to be a "liberation from the control of 'men in suits' ... it was to prove that people of less than middle age, without stiff collars or waistcoats, were capable of building and running an organisation".[25]

"Hey Jude" and *The White Album* were the first single and album, respectively, to be distributed with the Apple label affixed to each copy. However, none of the songs/recordings on either disk were the property of Apple Records; instead they belonged to the Beatles' contractual label, EMI/Capitol Records. The Apple label, therefore, was only a branding device in the case of the Beatles' own music. The Beatles did, however, act as producers for other musicians under the Apple label and, in those cases, the label indicated rights ownership. Even though John Lennon, in a letter to the radical paper *Black Dwarf*, stated his intention that Apple Records would be an example of workers regaining ownership of the means of production, the Beatles declined to release recordings by their signed band Goldfinger on the grounds that they believed that the music was insufficiently commercial.[26] While the Beatles did object to their own music being associated with other people's products, they were amenable regarding the advertising use of the groups they managed: in 1969; Apple released a label sampler EP sponsored by Walls Ice Cream.

The "Hey Jude/Revolution" single was advertised along with three other records by new Apple artists: Jackie Lomax, Mary Hopkin, and the Black Dyke Mills Brass Band. Thus, at the time of its debut, the hard-rock "Revolution" was itself used to advertise, promote, and brand other musical products in the Apple line. The Beatles ran these same ads in both the radical and trade press. Perhaps this was merely marketing the Beatles' music to a good target – but it could be taken as their attempt to support the radical movement by putting ads in its newspapers.

Within a year of founding, the Beatles themselves were struggling for control over their corporation. The Apple Boutique, a London shop that sold clothing and other items, had failed, and Paul had painted "Revolution" on its blacked-out windows – not as protest graffiti, but as an advertisement for the single.

The Response

In the weeks before "Hey Jude/Revolution" came out, critics' columns and consumer letters discussed the Beatles' past work and hashed over the rumours flying around about the soon-to-be-released music. In these passages, we learn that Beatles' songs were subject to two pieces of conventional wisdom: one was that the Beatles could sell anything with their name on it, and the other was that individual songs were puzzling at first, but "grew on you".[27] Thus, the Beatles were leading the *troc* and pushing the horizons of expectation in a way that taught their audience to engage in active interpretation.

When "Hey Jude/Revolution" appeared, there was little comment about the B-side in popular press reviews. Except for *Time* magazine's approval of the message of "Revolution" ("telling radical activists the world over to cool it"),[28] music critics focused on the longer, more experimental piece. After reviewing "Hey Jude", for example, *Record Mirror* simply wrote: "flipside: pacier, punchy, but on a less spectacular scale",[29] while *Record Retailer* said: "flip: faster, more compact".[30] Commentary on "Revolution" focused on the music rather than the lyrics: "I thought I had a bad pressing but subsequently found out that was the way it was supposed to sound because the Beatles say this is the sound of revolution, discordant ... If it wasn't so distorted it would be a tremendous number".[31]

Public response appears split. When *Melody Maker* dismissed "Revolution" ("The B-side is a fuzzy mess and best forgotten"), a letter in the next "Mailbag" said: "to call 'Revolution' a fuzzy mess is something akin to calling a Turner seascape a 'blur.' It is, but that is hardly the point. Look deeper and listen harder, please."[32] Consumers responding to a BBC Radio 1 poll commented only on the B-side's rock form: "'Revolution' is more in the Beatles' older style – which I prefer"; "'Revolution'? That's a drag, I don't really like it. Too much rock 'n' rolly and not as good as 'Lady Madonna'".[33]

Sociologists and musicologists, speculating on the public response to protest music, have remarked that the young of 1968 did not listen to or understand the lyrics.[34] Yet it is not clear that most students of the late 1960s were committed to total revolution in the way that today's academics often take for granted. For example, in the build-up to the Columbia University sit-in, student counter-protests took place, with one placard reading "Order is Peace!",[35] while a large-sample poll taken in 1970 among American high-school and college students found a desire for change, but also faith in the current system to bring about that change. Their heroes included Robert F. Kennedy, Bill Cosby, John Wayne, and Neil Armstrong, but the men they least admired were Fidel Castro, Eldridge Cleaver, George Wallace, and Ho Chi Minh – the majority, seemingly, rejected the far poles of the political spectrum.[36] Perhaps, then, "Revolution" was a pretty accurate reflection of many students' actual position: "You say you want a revolution – well, you know, we all want to change the world ... But if you go carrying pictures of Chairman Mao, you ain't gonna make it with anyone anyhow."

When *The White Album* was released, the popular press response was positive; some leaned toward "snow-blinded ecstasy".[37] Critics often glossed several cuts, but few commented on "Revolution 1". One who did declared it to be a "bluesy, gentler version" of the single, and added "it's different, softer, with the words clearer". But, echoing the response of most reviewers, he found "Revolution Number 9" beyond the horizon of expectation: "There is, in fact, no music in this cacophony of sound: the sort of noise you get when you spin the selection along the short wave at two in the morning. Noisy, boring and meaningless, which can only be some private joke for the Beatles' inner circle".[38] Here we can see the angry frustration caused by an unintelligible intention. If reading were simply a matter of creating individuated meanings out of whole cloth, such frustrations would not occur; it is only because reading normally rests on a plausible inference of intent that calls against private jokes are made. And, in fact, the meanings behind Beatles songs were sometimes intentionally cryptic; even *The White Album*'s printed insert admittedly included "arcane touches which only the Beatles' more intimate associates were likely to smile at".[39] Thus, with *The White Album* a new tension emerged between the musicians and their fans: on the one hand, Lennon was irritated with the way some readers inferred esoteric or overly mystical meanings; on the other, fans complained that some works had only "private meanings"–that is, meanings where only the Beatles could know what was intended.

In contrast to the popular press, the radical media reacted fiercely against all versions of "Revolution". *Ramparts* declared: "'Revolution' preaches counter-revolution".[40] The *New Left Review* called it a "lamentable petty bourgeois cry of fear".[41] The *Village Voice* wrote: "It is puritanical to expect musicians, or anyone else, to hew the proper line. But it is reasonable to request that they do not go out of their way to oppose it. Lennon has and it takes much of the pleasure out of their music for me."[42] The *Berkeley Barb* sneered, "'Revolution' sounds like the hawk plank adopted in the Chicago convention of the Democratic Death Party".[43] *Black Dwarf* railed, dismissing the song as "no more revolutionary than Mrs. Dale's Diary" (Lennon responded: "I don't remember saying Revolution was revolutionary–fuck Mrs Dale") and described Lennon as corrupted by his Apple business interests and no longer representing "rebellion, or love, or poetry, or mysticism but Big Business".[44]

Consistently, the leftist press held up the Stones' "Street-Fighting Man" as the preferred stance and called to the Beatles to convert. However, arguably it was the left who were not listening when "Street-Fighting Man" became their exemplar. Looking at these lyrics today, Mick Jagger's radical intention seems dubious: "Hey! think the time is right for a palace revolution / But where I live the game to play is compromise solution / Well, then what can a poor boy do / Except to sing for a rock 'n' roll band / Cause in sleepy London town / There's no place for a street fighting man." The Who's "Won't Get Fooled Again" has lyrics that are, arguably, sceptical about revolution too ("meet the new boss; same as the old boss"). All three British bands seem to take similarly ambivalent views, or at least detached positions, to the plausibility of radical upheaval.

From the beginning, some leftist critics also worked hard to make "Revolution" their own by emphasising the music over the lyrics. Greil Marcus claimed, "The music contained a message of its own, a message of excitement and freedom, which works against the sterility and repression in the lyrics", adding: "The music doesn't say 'cool it' or 'don't fight the cops.'"[45] Michael Wood, in *Commonweal*, tried to read the doo-wop treatment of "Revolution 1" as an irony undercutting the anti-revolutionary attitude of the lyrics.[46] In a flight of imaginative fancy, another commentator claimed:

> In this one, of course, The Beatles are simply telling the Maoists that Fabian gradualism is working, and that the Maoists might blow it all by getting the public excited before things are ready for "Revolution." The song makes it perfectly clear that the Beatles are on the side of, and working for, "Revolution" – and their war is going to be successful (it's gonna be alright). In short, "Revolution" takes the Moscow line against Trotskyites and the Progressive Labor Party, based on Lenin's "Leftwing

Extremism: An Infantile Disorder".[47]

Overall, however, 1968's radicals felt "Revolution" rejected their position that peaceful means were inadequate and that the time for action, even violence, had come.

Nina Simone responded to "Revolution" by adapting the song and parodying the lyrics to write a new song that represented a direct response to it. For example, in answer to Lennon's rejection of "minds that hate", Simone sang: "I know they'll say I'm preachin' hate / But if I have to swim the ocean / Well I would just to communicate / It's not as simple as talkin' jive / The daily struggle just to stay alive". At the outmost reaches of the interpretive community, however, an extreme reading prevailed. Charles Manson's "Family" parsed over every cut of *The White Album*, bending it to their own agenda:

> Listening to the White Album over and over again, in their drugged-out state, the Family's interpretations became even more bizarre ... But the song that really clinched the relationship was "Revolution 1." The lyric's mention of revolution and destruction fit snugly into Charlie's extremely elastic philosophy – that the time for peace and love was over, and now was the time for action.[48]

This was, of course, a similar message to that which the left was attributing to "Street-Fighting Man" – and the stance they were demanding of Lennon. However, when Manson went to trial for the brutal murder of Sharon Tate and her friends, the state did not consider the Beatles an accessory to the crimes, but instead saw the Manson family's interpretation of the songs as evidence of homicidal madness. It is elementary to acknowledge that in cases where culpability must be assigned, the test for a reading's validity is probable intent – whatever Manson heard in "Revolution 1", no prosecutor thought Lennon intended violence.

The Authors

The White Album arrived amid well-publicised creative squabbles in the band. It has often been seen, therefore, as a compilation "of separate egos, arguing for prominence".[49] The famous Lennon-McCartney duo collaborated for this work, but often in a perfunctory or adversarial fashion: "To Paul, John's new music seemed harsh, unmelodious and deliberately provocative. John, for his part, found Paul's songs cloyingly sweet and bland. For the first time, Lennon and McCartney saw no bridge between them."[50] Histories and biographies tell of conflicts and compromises with "Revolution". John preferred *The White Album* version; because the words were comprehensible, he felt the song was more political. The second version was recorded to please Paul, who thought the hard-rock beat was more commercial. The contention seems to have been a matter of bitterness for John, who later recalled:

> The first take of "Revolution" – well, George and Paul were resentful and said it wasn't fast enough. Now, if you go into the details of what a hit record is and isn't, maybe. But The Beatles could have afforded to put out the slow, understandable version of "Revolution" as a single, whether it was a gold record or a wooden record. But because they were so upset over the Yoko thing and the fact that I was becoming as creative and dominating as I had been in the early days, after lying fallow for a couple of years, it upset the applecart. I was awake again and they weren't used to it.[51]

The third version, "Revolution No. 9", was recorded by John and Yoko Ono, with assistance from George. John Lennon's affair with Yoko Ono also began in May of 1968; their first night was spent composing electronic music together. "Revolution No. 9" was one of the experiments in sound that the two played with extensively that summer. Lennon had now abandoned both his wife and his songwriting partner, going instead with the avant-garde artist. He expressed his relationship to Ono as complete identification: "She's me in drag".[52] Though the press was cruel to Yoko for years to follow, John's biographers now emphasise that they were close collaborators in both their art and their politics from that first moment.

Personal and professional conflict, therefore, weighed heavily on Lennon that spring. But the violence of the riots, and the rising pressure to become politically engaged, also preoccupied him. As the Beatles' biographer, Philip Norman, put it:

> John, in some obscure way, felt himself a part of this worldwide change from lisping hippy Love and Peace to brick-hurling activism ... Part of him wanted to be a pamphleteer, a rabble-rouser, a street fighter. The larger part was still buttoned into his Beatle self, still forged to a corporate smile, still fearful of what his Aunt Mimi might read about him in the press.[53]

This rather dismissive characterisation belies the sincerity with which Lennon seems to have struggled to formulate a responsible stance. In an interview with their "authorised biographer" Hunter Davies, given just before writing "Revolution", John elaborated on the public relations nightmare that had emerged after he compared the Beatles' popularity to that of Jesus:

> When I made the Jesus remark, lots of people sent me books about Jesus. I read a lot of them and found out things. I've found out, for example, that the Church of England isn't very religious. There's too much politics. You can't be both. You can't be powerful *and* pure. Perhaps I'll find out that the gurus are like that as well, full of politics. I don't know. All I know is that I am being made more aware by it all. I just want to be told more.[54]

In the same interview, he responds to barbs about his money: "I feel I could give up all this. It does waste a lot of energy. I have to wait and see what I'd be giving it up for, what I was replacing it for. I might give up all this material stuff in the end. But at the moment I want to find myself." We can see here themes of "Revolution": wanting to see a plan, to avoid hate, to free his own mind, change his own head.

Hunter Davies' *The Beatles: The Authorised Biography* was published in late summer that year. Some critics applauded the way Davies filled out the public's understanding of the young men who formed the Beatles in a desperate attempt to escape their working-class circumstances, thus "[allowing] us to see the young musicians for the first time as interesting, fallible, corporeal creatures". Lennon, in particular, seems to have been motivated by the promise of wealth: "I had to be a millionaire. If I couldn't do it without being crooked, then I'd have to be crooked".[55] Others focused on Lennon's assertions that he was "conning" the public through his music:

> I suppose I'm so indifferent about our music because other people take it so seriously. It can be pleasing in a way, but most of the time it gets my back up. ... It just takes a few people to get going, and they con themselves into thinking it's important. ... We're a con as well. We know we're conning them, because we know people want to be conned. They've given us the freedom to con them. Let's stick that in there we say, that'll start them puzzling. I'm sure all artists do, when they realise it's a con.[56]

After admissions like that, it would have been easy to dismiss everything Lennon wrote as "a con" meant to garner wealth. But with regard to revolutionary politics, his other public comments suggested a troubled earnestness. After "Revolution" was released and the radical press reacted, the editors of *Black Dwarf* published a letter criticising Lennon, advocating violent destruction, lauding "Street-Fighting Man", and asking the Beatles to join the movement. Lennon wrote back: "I don't worry about what you, the left, the middle, the right or any fucking boys club think. I'm not that *bourgeois*. I'm not only up against the establishment but you too." He reiterated the position he had taken in "Revolution": "I'll tell you what's wrong with the world: people – so do you want to destroy them? Until you/we change our head – there's no chance. Tell me of one successful revolution. Who fucked up communism, Christianity, capitalism, Buddhism, etc.? Sick heads, and nothing else." He ends by comparing constructive change with the destructive mission the letter advocated, "You smash it – and I'll build around it".[57]

An alternative understanding of the politics of "Revolution" might be related to what is now known as "acid communism"; a particular political sensibility that linked Sixties radicals with the psychedelic experiments of the counterculture. The tactics of "acid communism" mostly comprised of raising consciousness, firstly of individuals, then of society as a whole, and these tactics were typically pursued via techniques of self-transformation like yoga, meditation, veganism, sexuality, and drug consumption. As Jeremy Gilbert explains, while these specific acts may have no inherent political value and can easily become "banal distractions" enabling individuals to cope with alienation without ever challenging the structural source of those problems, there is nonetheless a confluence between the idea of "higher" consciousness as expressed within these mystical and yogic literature, and the idea of politically "raised" consciousness of more direct radicalism.[58] Gilbert writes:

> Both of these ideas had older antecedents. The idea of raised political consciousness had its roots in the Marxist idea of "class consciousness", whereby workers come to realise that their shared interests as workers are more significant than their private interest as individuals, or the cultural differences they may have with other workers. The mystical idea of "higher" ("elevated", "universal" or "cosmic") consciousness has its roots in Hindu and Buddhist ideas that the individual self is

an illusion. Escape from that illusion, realisation that the self is only an incidental element of a wider cosmos, is sometimes referred to as "enlightenment", but the original Sanskrit and pali terms might be better translated as "awoken".[59]

Read as an expression of "acid communism", we might say that Lennon was not so much making a reactionary denunciation of the violent upheaval of 1968 as offering an alternative political intervention.

While scholars like Jeremy Gilbert and Mark Fisher might endeavour to valorise some of the radical potential "acid communism" held, it is nonetheless a problematic stance within leftist politics. Terry Eagleton, for example, is especially dismissive, and given the extraordinary wealth enjoyed by the Beatles while they thoughtfully contemplated "all the lonely people", his words hold a particular resonance:

> People who have a surplus of material goods are likely to resort to bogus forms of spirituality as a much-needed refuge from them. A gullible belief in wood nymphs, magic crystals, Theosophy or alien spacecraft is simply the flipside of their worldliness. It is no wonder that Tarot, packaged occultism and ready-to-serve transcendence should be so fashionable in the Hollywood hills. The spiritual in this view is not a specific mode of materiality—a question of feeding the hungry, welcoming the stranger, falling in love, celebrating friendship, speaking up for justice and so on—but a flight from such drearily mundane matters. It offers you a welcome respite from a glut of minders, agents, hair stylists and heated swimming pools. It represents the bad faith of the fabulously rich.[60]

Whatever one's stance on "acid communism", we can certainly see themes of awareness raising recur throughout Beatles' lyrics, which, particularly around the period when "Revolution" was written, often exhort listeners to share their spiritual awareness. For example, in "Within You, Without You", George encourages us to "try to realise it's all within yourself", while several songs want to "take (us) away" such as "Magical Mystery Tour", "Strawberry Fields Forever", and "Lucy in the Sky with Diamonds". Throughout the Beatles' post-1965 oeuvre, love is purported as the basis for a total and satisfying philosophy of life.[61] Arguably, "All You Need is Love" most directly articulates the radical potential of love as *the* answer to all of life's problems, and given that the song begins with the "Marseillaise" – an anthem to freedom and a revolutionary song if ever there was one – we might listen to "All You Need is Love" alongside "Revolution" as similarly inclined political songs.

Indeed, to note the significance of the "Marseillaise" at the beginning of "All You Need is Love" is to allow the song a symbolic meaning very distinct from that exclusively provided in the lyrics and therefore recognise that the meaning of a piece of music is not constituted by verbal and literary properties alone. To this end, the various iterations of "Revolution" might each be understood as constituting very different forms of political statement. As already noted, rock critics like Greil Marcus argued that the aggressive arrangement and distortion of the fast version juxtaposes the "repressed" lyrics. This poses the problem of how political content exists within pieces of music. For example, John Scannell's music biography of James Brown explores the affective capacity of Brown's music as an assemblage: that is, an apparatus for the production of a particular type of sonic and aesthetic affect that causes certain intensifications of bodies and creates a shared embodied affective event.[62] In other words, the political content of music might register at a far more somatic level and therefore it would be entirely a mistake to regard the lyrics alone as constituting the song's politics. Given the ambiguity of the various recordings of "Revolution", we might conclude that "Revolution" should be simultaneously understood as valorising *and* rejecting radical violent action.

Interestingly, Scannell argues that we must understand

the "propulsive drive" of James Brown's music as charged by the dynamism of the civil rights era, and that therefore we should hear the music as an aesthetic reflection of the broader existential conditions that Brown was rendering in musical form. Arguably, however, contextualising "Revolution" within the maelstrom of 1968 is a far more complicated affair than contextualising James Brown within the American civil rights movement. This is because the meaning of 1968 and the ideas of revolution during the various radical events of the year remain deeply contested. As Kristin Ross argues, the actual events of 1968 have been overtaken by their representations; despite the clear grounding of some of the foremost movements of 1968 in Marxist politics and anti-imperialist objections to the American war in Vietnam, a common but deeply problematic narrative holds that the year's radical politics should be understood as the libidinal explosion of no-longer-to-be repressed youth – and therefore a political struggle that came to be consummated in the rise of baby-boomer consumer culture.[63] This means that trying to clarify the political meaning of "Revolution" by referring to the broader political phenomena of 1968 only produces more waves of ambiguity and contestation. Perhaps the safest conclusion is that "Revolution" is a song that cannot be read beyond its ambiguities.

"Revolution" was nevertheless the first in a string of Lennon songs that were directly political. Most reflect his self-image as a "peacenik"; when Pete Seeger introduced "Give Peace a Chance" at the 1969 March on Washington, it was declared that "the peace movement has at last found its anthem".[64] But by 1970, Lennon was reinventing himself as a radical songwriter. In an interview for *Red Mole*, he stressed how "Revolution 1" had said "count me in" but concluded that "Revolution" was a mistake: "The mistake was that it was anti-revolution".[65] In his newfound revolutionary mode, he arrived in New York wearing a Mao badge, joining Chicago Seven defendants Jerry Rubin and Abbie Hoffman, and sharing a stage with Black Panther founder Bobby Seale. By 1972 Lennon had composed "Power to the People": "Say you want a revolution / We better get on right away / Well you get on your feet / And out on the street / Singing power to the people." The album *Some Time in New York City* (also 1972) contained lyrics like "free all prisoners everywhere", "leave Ireland for the Irish", and "woman is the nigger of the world".

Lennon seemed intent on rehabilitating the Beatles politically. In one interview, he said, "I resent the implication that the Stones are the revolutionaries and that the Beatles weren't, you know? If the Stones were, or are, [then] the Beatles *really* were. They're not in the same class, music-wise or power-wise. Never were."[66]

Later biographies and films have taken divergent views of this period in Lennon's life. Jon's Wiener's *Come Together*,[67] for instance, describes Lennon as radically committed until the Nixon administration's attempts to deport him wore him down. Amazon currently lists more than a dozen DVDs on John Lennon, most of which focus on his years as a revolutionary. Other historians dismiss this period as one of Lennon's typically intense swings of interest or alliance.[68] As a consequence of all this intentional reading (and, of course, as a result of the true complexity of his actual life), Lennon has left contradictory legends. Hunter Davies argues that, in England, Lennon is remembered as a loveable, if cranky and eccentric, pop millionaire, but in the US, as a revolutionary and a radical.[69] Lennon's own propensity to change positions, to play with the public's readings, or to seed cryptic lines in his songs, have left a record from which these dramatically different views can beeasily assembled.

Nevertheless, in the last interview he gave, six hours before his assassination, Lennon returned to "Revolution": "The lyrics stand today. They're still my feeling about politics: I want to see the *plan*. That is what I used to say to Abbie Hoffman and Jerry Rubin. Count me out if it's for violence. Don't expect me on the barricades unless it is with flowers."[70]

Significance

"Revolution" is important as one of a subgenre of 1960s protest songs and as the ambiguous beginning of Lennon's later corpus as a political singer. *The White Album*, on which two versions appeared, is significant, for entirely different reasons, to both the Beatles' oeuvre and the pop genre as a whole. While earlier Beatles' albums were also experimental, ironic, and eclectic, *The White Album* is said to represent their apotheosis, specifically for its brash appropriation of musical styles and its insouciant subversion of original purposes. From "Back in the USSR" to "Rocky Raccoon", the borrowed styles seem to flaunt their disloyalty to historical intent. "With its vast cornucopia of styles, the *White Album* suggests that the Beatles don't play pop music–they own it. ... Other bands might occasionally dare to pastiche some other kind of music. The Beatles just went in and grabbed it."[71] This brazen borrowing, however, is the key to *The White Album*'s significance to the *troc*. As David Quantik puts it:

> This is the legacy of the White Album, the gift it gave to popular music. It freed millions of bands from the tyranny of genre, the narrow-minded attitude that says, this band shall be a soul group and this band shall be a rock group. The White Album showed the world that pop music was for the taking, and the world never looked back.[72]

Stepping back from *The White Album*, we are faced with the significance of the Beatles and their work as a whole. This, of course, is impossible to overstate, but crucial to articulate. The Beatles' ability to imagine and perform beyond the conventional limits of their genre is a factor, but one must also give due credit to the formal complexity and sophistication of many of their works. Importantly, the Beatles' artistry, much like Pop Art and other schools of the 1960s (such as the Fluxus movement, of which Yoko Ono was a part), often purposely played with traditional boundaries between commerce, popular culture, and art, as if to question their separate existence.[73] Ultimately, though it grew out of a lightweight, popular genre, the Beatles' music became canonical. In the 1996 preface to his biography, Hunter Davies described a scene in the British Museum:

> Beside the glass-topped tables displaying the works of Shakespeare, Dickens, Wordsworth, Keats, and other assorted and long dead great figures, you will see a table containing ten original Beatles songs, in their own fair hand writing. On most days, the largest crowd in the room is around that table. … The reason for all this reverence, which would have struck most people as risible back in 1968, is simple: their music.[74]

The Beatles had a profound effect on culture across the world in the 1960s, but that impact deepened over the next few decades, eventually reaching the level of admiration that endures – and where the music, in some sense, belongs to everyone; as Davies puts it: "now it is universally accepted that the Beatles gave us almost 200 popular songs which will be remembered as long as the world has any breath left to hum the tunes."[75]

Clearly, the passage of time has added a further layer of meaning and depth of intensity to the Beatles' catalogue as they transform into objects of nostalgia that triggered subjective meanings for listeners. It is interesting, therefore, to jump forward two decades, from Sixties "hippy culture" to Eighties "yuppy culture", and to explore how the same song mutates in the public mind. In the 1980s, as we now explore, "Revolution" was not only to be recontextualised by becoming an object of nostalgia, but also by its re-surfacing at the zenith of 1980s consumer culture, as the background music for a Nike ad.

Chapter Three
The Shoe

John Lennon was shot to death outside his home at the Dakota in New York City on December 8, 1980. This tragic event was a fit opening to the decade: commentators have since cast the 1980s as a period representing the inversion of the social consciousness and radical fervour of the 1960s. The generation that had challenged the materialistic, militaristic values of their parents morphed into super-consumers. Prominent "sell outs" were everywhere. "Yuppie", the pejorative that denoted the consumer ethic of erstwhile flower children, was first used in print to describe the Eighties identity of former Chicago Seven radical Jerry Rubin, by then a businessman. Bobby Seale, founder of the Black Panthers, started a barbeque franchise that included a book, *Barbeque'n with Bobby*, a television show, and, now, a DVD, while his comrade, Eldridge Cleaver, joined the Republicans. The Rolling Stones issued their own Visa card and the Who pioneered sponsored tours with the "Schlitz Brewery Farewell Tour" of 1982.

A huge hit movie of the early decade was *The Big Chill*, a sentimental look at the angst of the "Make Love Not War" generation, punctuated by familiar hits from the 1960s. A blogger writing today remembers:

The Big Chill is about my peers. When first released in 1983, I, like the characters, was in my early thirties, a former rebellious collegian from the '60s. After a decade in the work-a-day world, being a family man and raising babies, watching *The Big Chill* was like a fantastic time machine and took me back to places long forgotten. It really connected with me on a visceral level and I loved it.[1]

The Big Chill soundtrack sold as well as the movie tickets: one of several in that decade–from *Fame* to *Flashdance* to *Footloose*– to do so.

The marriage between music, film, and commerce was traceable to the emergence of MTV, a new cable network featuring wall-to-wall TV commercials for pop music. At first, musicians merely sang their songs for the camera, but soon artists like Madonna and Michael Jackson acted out or choreographed elaborate productions–and young producers raced toward the new medium, pushing for the music video to be taken seriously as art.[2] The resulting genre claimed distinctive styles, from grainy, black-and-white films to jumpy montages of highly saturated colour, to elaborate claymation scenarios. Music videos, at once art and advertisement, were celebrated by some for their distinctively postmodern qualities, but feared by others who saw rock as resistance and television as the embodiment of mainstream commerce.

The "fitness craze" was another element of the zeitgeist that further blurred whatever boundaries existed between commerce, video, and pop music–and between all of these and athletics. First jogging, and then aerobics, exploded onto the scene. The tights, leg warmers, and shoes that were fashionable for aerobics classes were also worn on the street. As much dance as exercise, aerobics classes invariably involved loud, thumping rock in the background. Workout videos flooded the market for those who couldn't make it to one of the new fitness clubs. Jane Fonda (known by some as "Hanoi Jane" in the 1960s) hawked an extremely successful string of aerobics videos and clubs. Circling back, the clothes, music, and shoes became a popular film and soundtrack, *Flashdance*, which in turn was translated to and parodied in various music videos – and imitated by ads.

From the beginning, MTV's commercial foundation was extended by advertisers aping the style of the music video. The California Raisin Advisory Board had a hit with claymation raisins singing "I Heard It Through the Grapevine". Levi's 501 jeans reestablished claims to the baby-boomer's bottoms through blue-tinted, hand-held montages set to blues. But advertising was viewed with suspicion, especially on university campuses, where the left often persisted, despite the consumerism and conservatism of the Age of Reagan. In this intellectual milieu, the first body of academic advertising criticism grew, led by Judith Williamson, and followed by Sut Jhally and others. Here, too, the influence of commercial video was felt when a cottage industry sprang up to produce cultural criticism of advertising in video form for university use. The first of these was Jean Kilbourne's aforementioned 1978 *Killing Us Softly*,[3] which took a large number of ads and accused the advertisers behind them of social crimes. One tactic peculiar to the emergent genre was to attribute an intention to imbed sexual imagery into the ads, leading quickly to implications that disguised dirty pictures would make consumers buy (Kilbourne's videos do this, but the best example is 1992's *The Ad and the Id*, a bizarre film produced by Berkeley's continuing education centre).[4] Yet, in parallel to the academy's appetite for exposing its hegemonic discourses, advertising of the 1980s experienced a renaissance of creative form markedly influenced by the innovations in music video.

The Troc

The advertising *troc* of the 1980s is now recognised as one of the three most creative periods in the century, a time in which advertising moved closer to art.[5] During the 1920s, the 1960s, and the 1980s, advertising showed formal changes reflective of styles and standards often thought typical of art – and, through these innovations, reached new levels of effectiveness. In each period, a vanguard of creative people emerged to argue for, theorise, and produce a set of exemplary texts.

The creative leaders of the 1980s saw themselves as working in the tradition of the "Creative Revolution" of the 1960s, declaring themselves disciples of Bill Bernbach, the iconoclastic founder of Doyle Dane Bernbach, which produced iconic campaigns (Avis, Volkswagen) in the 1960s. The hallmarks of the Bernbach approach, as stated by him and as carried forward by his followers, were to approach the consumer with respect rather than condescension, to produce ads that were witty or artistic rather than irritating or bland, and to stand up to the client in defence of this mission, even if it meant losing the business. So Bernbach's approach was explicitly both artistic and adversarial – and claimed authorship for agency over client.

Remember that the *troc* shows the forward-leaning aspects of the genre, but also implies a response to, sometimes a reaction against, the past. In both the 1960s and the 1980s, the reaction was against the science of market research and the sycophantic attitude of the "hack marketing people" (by the 1980s, often known simply as "the suits") toward their clients. The Bernbach school had pitted itself against the Unique Selling Proposition and other 1950s concepts developed by Rosser Reeves, whose philosophy demeaned consumers and was product-centred in a narrowly "rational" way. His views nearly always resulted in grating, repetitive ads. So, the science of research and the business attitude were seen by the Bernbach school as factors that inevitably produced ugly, insulting, disingenuous ads.

The Bernbach school agencies of the 1980s consistently refused to do copy research; the brands they built, including Nike, went along with the risk. Indeed, many agencies and clients of the era were proud of taking chances, often arguing that eschewing research helped them to reach the creative breakthroughs they wanted. The reactive aspects of the 1980s creative surge also included a pull away from New York as the centre of the advertising industry. The most outstanding spots, most admired creatives, and most talked-about shops were either on the West Coast of the US (Chiat/Day, Hal Riney, Goodby, Silverstein), or in its heartland (Fallon McElligott, GSD&M).

Chiat/Day's Lee Clow, whose "1984" spot for Macintosh is still heralded on industry lists, played a pivotal role with Nike. In his interview with the *Smithsonian*, he described his early career in terms that explicitly reference this Bernbach-oriented trajectory:

> Right at the time I was getting up to speed in terms of an advertising career, this [Bernbach] stuff was being done. I said, "Hey this can be fun if you operate in the world of advertising with some respect for the people you're talking to. And you don't use the old rules of just kinda grinding people into buying your soap." So I just got kinda excited when I was at Ayer about doing great stuff and Ayer is one of those more traditional agencies who[se] priorities are more: "This is business, it is not an art." And so I looked around in L.A. Jay Chiat and Guy Day were the two people that were trying to do it like Doyle Dane Bernbach was doing it.[6]

Clow went to Chiat/Day, where he created some of the most admired—and effective—campaigns of the next twenty years.

The essential capital of any advertising agency is its creative people. The risk of losing good personnel to an agency that allows them more creative expression, as Ayer lost Clow to Chiat/Day, is a constant pressure that must be balanced against pleasing a too-controlling client. Furthermore, the model begun in the 1960s for a pair of disaffected creatives to leave the big agency and start their own shop—while taking their best clients with them—was still in force: Mary Wells Lawrence, George Lois, Carl Ally, and others of the Creative Revolution had taken this tack. The need for agencies to retain stars like Clow became more pressing in the 1980s as advertisers flocked to small, innovative houses in search of creative genius. So, in order to keep creative capital, agency managers had to attend to the rewards of the *troc* that went beyond higher sales and salaries. For the creative staff, recognition as a member of an elite creative community – to be seen as one of the "stars" like Lee Clow – was highly desired. Such stars commanded more attention and bigger salaries, but they were also rewarded with more creative control and choice over projects. Intangibles like nurturing talent and support for new techniques became crucial.

The watermarks of the 1980s *troc* for advertisements are now identifiable. In addition to the MTV visual style and the use of music, there was a strong tendency toward irony, parody, and pastiche. Most salient to observers at the time was the tendency to avoid product shots, to use oblique taglines, even to minimise the appearance of the logo. The leading-edge advertisements used few jingles or demos. Many were even cryptic, as in the Infiniti spots, which seemed more like haiku than ads. Wordplay, as in the J&B or Nynex ads, was a frequent focus. There was also a trend toward playing with images, sounds, and words previously held to be "sacred" or outside the bounds of commerce, as in the Absolut Vodka ads (art), the Bennetton ads (politics), or the Fallon-McElligott ads for the Episcopal Church (religion).

The Product

Nike began in the early 1960s as Blue Ribbon Sports, originally distributing running shoes for a Japanese company. It was the creation of Phil Knight, a former runner at the University of Oregon, and Bill Bowerman, who had been a track coach. In the late 1970s, the emergent jogging trend drove sales of their running shoes from $10 million to $270 million a year.[7] In 1971, Blue Ribbon Sports changed its corporate name to Nike, and by 1978, Jon Anderson had won the Boston Marathon, Jimmy Conners had won Wimbledon and the US Open, and Henry Rono had set four track and field records; all wearing Nikes.[8] The Nike leadership was extremely focused on performance athletics and very product-feature oriented; the corporate culture was also white and patriarchal. They were, to say the least, sure of

60

themselves. As Knight was to later describe the organisation: "In the early days, when we were just a running company and almost all our employees were runners, we understood the consumer very well. There is no shoe school, so where do you recruit people for a company that develops and markets running shoes? The running track. It made sense, and it worked. We and the consumer were one and the same."[9]

It is perhaps not surprising that this management missed the trend that nearly destroyed them: the popularity of women's aerobics, and a fashionable look to go with it. Instead, that advantage went to Reebok, a British shoemaker who produced a soft leather shoe that was pretty, comfortable, and strong enough for aerobics, if not for distance running. From the time Reebok introduced its Freestyle shoe in 1982, their sales rose from $3.5 million to $65 million in 1984, and then to a staggering $307 million in 1987.[10] The shoes, available in high tops and multiple colours, became salient in the cultural landscape, worn as often as a fashion statement as for sports. For instance, when Cybill Shepherd collected her 1985 Emmy for the wildly popular TV series, *Moonlighting*, she strode across the stage in a black strapless evening gown and a pair of orange high-top Reeboks.

Nike began to lose sales, face layoffs, and endure the untold embarrassment of falling style points. The problem was not product design: Nike produced an unambiguously superior shoe from a performance vantage, but it was not hip enough for the style-conscious milieu of the 1980s. Faced with the need to up the company's cool quotient, Nike's Phil Knight did what CEOs in such a dilemma often do—he began to look for a "hot shop" advertising agency. While his production and design people worked to ready a new line of colourful shoes with an air bubble gimmick in the heel, Knight announced that the Nike account was up for review.

The Authors

Given Nike's current global image, it is somewhat difficult to accept the frequent observation by those who were there at the beginning that its management, especially Phil Knight and his co-founder Bill Bowerman, originally saw themselves as mavericks, even as revolutionaries. Knight was as suspicious of advertising as any leftist academic, considering it "largely a waste of money and a fraud".[11] Ironically, given what came later, Phil Knight resisted the pull to engage in marketing, believing that sports were a sacred space and should not be contaminated by commercialisation. His first words to admen Dan Wieden and David Kennedy when they met in 1980 were: "Hi, I'm Phil Knight and I hate advertising." At that time, the creative team, two "long-haired, bearded flower children", were employed at John Brown Advertising in Seattle.[12] For two years, Weiden and Kennedy wrote the straightforward, product-oriented copy Knight wanted, confined mostly to print because Knight didn't trust television. Then, in 1982, they left the agency where they worked to start their own, taking Nike as their only client.

Unfortunately, that very next year, Nike decided to put its business up for review. They invited Chiat/Day of Los Angeles and Hal Riney of San Francisco, both known Bernbach school agencies, to participate in the pitch, but also graciously included little Weiden+Kennedy. In the end, Nike liked Chiat/Day best, because "the agency was being heralded as an up-and-coming creative force with an attitude", because of the buzz from their Macintosh work, and because they admired Lee Clow.[13] The account was subsequently split between the two agencies, with Chiat taking the more glamorous image mission, and Weiden+Kennedy keeping the day-to-day product advertising. Wieden and Kennedy, who must have thought they would "share in Nike's inevitably glowing future", were suddenly diminished, while "all the glory stuff" went to the new agency.[14] The message was clear: Nike did not think W+K could produce cool enough work to help with the image problem, so they were going for "more imaginative advertising" with one of that era's hottest shops.[15]

The Nike team also felt that they had a match with Lee Clow, and both organisations felt their cultures were similar. Clow recalls: "When they came to us finally, they said, 'We don't want a bunch of account executives.' Yeah, we were culturally a very similar company. They said, 'We don't want a bunch a guys shufflin' around in suits, you know, with a bunch of strategy documents, because that's bullshit."[16] Although Nike's management wanted the expertise a sophisticated agency could give them, they were untutored in the protocol for dealing with high-end creatives. Not only did the Nike men force their own campaign idea for the 1984 Olympics ("I Love LA") on the agency, they insisted on choosing the media and markets themselves. The marketing team was led by Rob Strasser, who was "controversial" inside Nike; the agency "felt characters like Strasser would have driven 90 per cent of the agencies in America berserk."[17]

Under Strasser's bulldozing style, Chiat/Day was left only with full authorship for an outdoor campaign celebrating the 1984 Olympics. This they produced in legendary form, putting up huge painted action portraits of athletes over freeways and on the sides of buildings. These dramatic images – "It's so simple, it's art", in the words of the *LA Times* – were news all over the country and led many to think Nike, not Converse, was the official shoe sponsor of the 1984 Olympics.[18] The Los Angeles Olympics were the first games where the sponsoring city refused to underwrite the costs; therefore, the organisers hustled corporate sponsorships as never before, eventually turning a profit for the event.[19] In the process, however, the games became heavily commercialised, and within this setting, Nike's huge, hand-painted billboards with only a tiny logo to identify them seemed to take the high road.[20] Between the positive response to the beauty of the signs and moral approval for the low-profile brand identification, Nike received a great deal of free publicity: "the message is such a soft sell, and the photographs are so distinct that they could be mistaken for, well, *nice big pictures.*"[21] Furthermore, the boards were so different that Nike was credited with injecting new energy into an entire medium, as evidenced by one contemporaneous analyst from the journal *Madison Avenue*:

> Over the past decade or so, outdoor advertising has developed a reputation as an industry moribund to the point of catatonia. Outdated, boring, resistant to change – if not exactly accurate, such phrases were common when advertisers talked about outdoor. The general images of billboards and their kin was of a medium rooted not at all reluctantly in the past, a medium that had been satisfied to stand still while television, radio, and print raced into the future.[22]

When the agency won awards for the campaign and wanted, as is customary, to place recognition ads in newspapers, Nike's response was distinctly unlike a partner: Strasser vetoed it, saying that he "wanted to make damn sure Chiat/Day kept its name away from Nike when it came to the consumer."[23] Subsequently, when Jay Chiat was interviewed about the campaign on television, Nike executives became furious because he was "taking credit" for the work.[24] Nike management then could not understand why they suddenly had no access to Lee Clow.

Sales were still plummeting. The freefall that Nike was experiencing is best summed up via Knight's assessments each year: "Orwell was right. 1984 was a tough year"; "The best thing you can say about 1985 is that it's over"; and, in 1986, "The sad fact is that Nike's not a very good company".[25] Nike's new Air Jordan line, with Michael Jordan as an endorser and Chiat/Day commercials to glorify him, had been brought to market in 1985, but, after an initial bump in sales, the campaign and the product line, in Knight's words, "fell on its face".[26] As Nike's sales dropped, Reebok's quadrupled.[27]

Meanwhile, Wieden+Kennedy had gained national recognition

for a Honda scooter campaign by scoring the huge coup of Lou Reed as endorser, as well as the rights to his counterculture song, "Walk on the Wild Side" (in the ad Lou advised: "Hey, don't settle for walkin'"). And after appearances by Grace Jones and Miles Davis, Wieden+Kennedy had established themselves as an agency that could work the impossible. Nike, impressed by the Honda ads, frustrated that they had lost the attention of their new star, and disappointed in their results, "released" Chiat/Day from the relationship, citing, among other things, "style differences".[28] To that end, it is important to note how, for the advertising agency, benefits accrue from the attention generated within the industry itself; it is erroneous to assume that adverts are designed with the sole intention of selling commodities for the business that commissions them. Decades later, Wieden recalled the Lou Reed ad as the moment in which the agency "took off": "it was a very influential spot, even though it didn't get a ton of media weight. It made Nike, which had rightfully seen us as a small local shop, take us seriously, and it helped us gain the rest of the business back. It also sold a lot of scooters".[29]

Nike's internal correspondence regarding the decision to reassign the whole account to W+K makes it clear that this was not a straightforward case of leaving one agency because of poor results and seeking another, more effective group. Instead, these documents reveal a tension between wanting an agency that could provide objectivity and original creative ideas and one that would identify more with Nike's goals than their own. Nike was looking for control and loyalty, but realised that the tradeoff was "hot creative".[30] One anonymous memo remarks that Chiat's "spots have a stronger Chiat/Day identity than client identity. This may be the eventual goal of ad agencies but it's not for us".[31] Though Nike realised they would increasingly face a similar problem with W+K, the glow of the Honda campaign won out in the end.

Because advertising agencies' quest for creativity is often dismissed as silly and vain, it is important to reveal the financial considerations in play. Both Chiat/Day and Wieden+Kennedy were being paid on a commission-plus-fees basis. Both got 17% commission on media – but since Chiat/Day commanded television, their income from media was three times that of the smaller agency ($1.3 million versus $612,000 a year). Their fees showed a similar structure, with Chiat getting $1.5 million annually to W+K's $480,000.[32] Evidently, being the one who wins awards and accolades makes a big impact on the bottom line. Note also that lower pay and a smaller budget were allocated to the product-oriented ads, not the image campaign.

The idea for "Revolution" came from a "little wild card team" at W+K – two young women, one of whom was so junior that she was still responsible for answering the phones.[33] Twenty-four-year-old Janet Champ, who saw herself as a leftist-poet-reluctantly-turned-copywriter, was so inexperienced she was painfully aware that she might be a drag on her partner, Susan Hoffman. Champ tells how they went to lunch to brainstorm:

We went down to the Dakota [Café] and there's a picture they have of the Dakota, the apartment building. Right above our table. I mean we just happened to be seated at this table and there just happened to be this picture of the Dakota. And the funniest thing was I kept staring 'cause I'd always wanted this one picture of the apartment building and I was absolutely crazy about John Lennon. He was one of my biggest heroes. So I was thinking about him and I was looking at this picture and I was talking to Susan. And she kept saying, "What's the big deal about this – this shoe, what's really the story behind this shoe?" And I kept saying, "Well, I guess it's this revolutionary thing. They keep saying it's this revolutionary thing so that's what it is, it's a huge revolution." And Susan kept saying, "Well, doesn't that (snaps her fingers several times) *ring a bell?*" And, you know, I'm lookin' at the picture and I'm lookin' at Susan and I'm thinkin' "Is she thinkin' what I'm thinkin'"? But I didn't say anything. And she said, "Isn't there – isn't there a song?" And I said, "well, yeah, by the Beatles." And she said, "Well, why don't we–what about *that?*" And I'm thinkin' "I gotta answer the phones, but sure if you think that's a great idea, let's go do it." I mean, you know...[34]

They presented the idea to the agency principals that afternoon. "Actually Susan presented it by standing on top of the table and saying, 'This is great, this is great, you don't understand this is great.' And Dan and David, as they so often do, were sittin' with this look on their face like, 'We have no idea what you're talking about. What are you saying? You want to use the Beatles–are you crazy?'"[35] Dan Wieden recalls that when they reviewed all the ideas for the campaign, "of all the stuff we had–there was a lot of really powerful explanations, the benefits were there. But the one that you couldn't get out of your mind was that stupid 'Revolution.' And so we presented it, with a bit of trepidation, to the client." The client's response to the proposed campaign speaks volumes: "You've given me my Lou Reed".[36] This tells us that the campaign was about one-upping Honda and Chiat/Day, as much as overstepping Reebok; it was about egos as well as sales.

It is important to note how far the agency had departed from their original brief and how determined they were to present Nike with something extraordinary. As Scott Bedbury, who eventually became Nike's Creative Director, later recounted (and it is interesting to note how the contributions of Janet Champ and Susan Hoffman disappear from the story):

I was further surprised to learn that Nike had not specified in a brief that they were looking for anything even remotely resembling "Revolution" from their ad agency ... In fact, not wanting anything too razzle-dazzle to detract from their goal of showcasing its new "Vis-Air" technology, the client had originally indicated that it was looking for a far more straightforward product-oriented campaign. As a bemused

Wieden & Kennedy staffer later advised me, 'They were hoping for an extended shot of a shoe, on a rotating Susan, with a light shining through the air bag.' The genius of the agency had been to take that particular brief and run with it. ... The agency's principals, Dan Wieden and David Kennedy, decided on their own that they wanted to create a campaign that would break the mold, not just to conduct an abstract aesthetic exercise but to say something enduring and meaningful about the Nike brand.[37]

As it happened, a pair of new music video directors, Paula Grief and Peter Kagan, had just dropped off a reel for the agency to view.[38] The two had produced a run that included Duran Duran ("Notorious"), Steve Winwood ("Higher Love"), and Scritti Politi ("Perfect Way"). They were nominated at the 1987 Video Music Awards for best editing, best cinematography, and best art direction. They were clearly at the cutting edge of the MTV *troc* in 1987. W+K snapped them up for Nike and Peter Kagan and Paula Grief became the advertisement directors.

Today Grief and Kagan's videos look nearly identical to each other – and very much like other videos of the period. Each is composed of quick cuts between two kinds of shot: a shaky black-and-white view and dramatically lit (often backlit) colour footage. It's all "very Eighties". Peter Kagan characterised their place in the *troc*: "Look at Russian icons on wood. The way this woman and child were depicted identically all over the country. People who had no idea it was happening somewhere else were doing it exactly the same way. Images arose out of that culture that were all homogeneous".[39] Note that this quotation shows that Kagan views himself as a kind of artist, even if working in a popular (or "folk") genre, like Russian icons. The style of production used for the ad was particularly unusual; the idiosyncratic effect was generated by projecting the grainy film against a wall and then videotaping the projection.[40] As Kagan recounted, the brief for the "Revolution" ad was to "create a feeling and not tell a story".[41]

Notes from a post-production meeting provide further insight into the negotiated intentionalities involved. The overall theme was a "revolution in fitness lifestyle", but it was about "feeling good", not "looking good"—so a frame with a "guy combing hair" was removed. "Unfortunately, NIKE is 'macho' company", the notes said, so the original opening frames, three shots of women, were eliminated ("but keep women in spot just don't begin w/").[42] Somewhat unusually, the production of the advertisement broke conventional advertising practice inasmuch as it was not a specifically storyboarded production. Scott Bedbury noted, "So much of what made the campaign memorable had been the result of a create-as-we-go, we'll-figure-it-all-out later attitude on the part of the creative team".[43] Perhaps reflecting this ad-hoc approach to production, and serving as a reminder that advertising production is often a highly contested practice, Grief and Kagan were to learn that they had become suddenly excluded from the production process:

A few weeks later Paula and I were in L.A. shooting a Duran Duran video on a soundstage that happened to be on the same backlot as—the editor that Wieden+Kennedy were using for their 'final' edit. What final edit? This was a first for us. No one had ever taken an edit away from us. We had always finished our stuff all the way to air. We went in and saw what they had done. I hated it. There were jump cuts that looked like what your dad would do to look cool. I felt like they were doing a lame imitation of Laura Israel. I might have had a bit of a tantrum ... They had taken the groovy little technique from my living room wall, and had some editor in L.A. mix it with stock footage.[44]

Meanwhile, client and agency agreed they did not want to use sound-a-likes, so the rights to both the song and the recording had to be obtained. While it was possible to use Beatles' songs for advertisements in the form of cover versions—for example, "We Can Work It Out" had been used for Hewlett-Packard computers; "With a Little Help From my Friends" by Gateway; "Taxman" by H&R Black tax advisers; and "When I'm 64" sung by Julian Lennon for All State Insurance—obtaining the rights to use a Beatles' original recording was another matter.[45] Remember that Apple Records had no direct rights in this matter—their label, a mere branding device on both the single and the album, masked the fact that Capitol/EMI owned the mechanical rights to the Beatles' recordings. In 1985, Michael Jackson had bought the performance rights to a whole catalogue of Beatles' songs, outbidding even Paul McCartney. Jackson's representative was predisposed toward allowing use of the song and voluntarily contacted Yoko Ono to pitch the idea, in order to be able to tell Jackson that Lennon's widow had approved the use. Ono endorsed the concept. Capitol/EMI, however, responded that "we will never, ever, consent to license of the Beatles music for an advertisement ... there isn't enough money out there for anyone to buy it."[46] But Ono intervened on behalf of Nike and a rough cut of the ad was sent to "a committee"—which Nike believed to include Ono, the remaining Beatles, and an Apple representative—at EMI for their approval.[47] Janet Champ recalled:

> [W]hat made me feel really good about having this spot was we wrote Yoko Ono and we went and told her what the idea was—I didn't get to go, but we sent the idea to her and we asked her what she thought about it—and she loved it ... And the Beatles were all behind it, too, so once they said it was all right, we felt pretty good about it.[48]

Yoko Ono, who was, in the minds of many, the best proxy for Lennon's own intentions, later explained to *Time* magazine that she didn't "want to see John deified" nor for "John's songs to be part of a cult of glorified martyrdom" – a cultural trend that had bothered her since his death.[49] She said she wanted the music to be enjoyed by "a new generation", "to make it part of their lives instead of a relic of the distant past".[50] As Mark Thomashow, one of the Nike management team recalled, Paul McCartney did not object to the license on the grounds that the song, composed by Lennon, was a matter for Yoko to decide.[51] Ringo Starr was appearing in ads for a wine cooler – standing beside a man in a polar bear suit – and so many have had no qualms about the commercialisation of "Revolution". In any case, at least in the minds of Nike and Weiden+Kennedy staff, legitimate permissions had been obtained, apparently with the advance approval of all the living Beatles, Yoko Ono, and Michael Jackson. The deal reportedly amounted to $250,000 for EMI and another $250,000 to SBK Entertainment World for the copyright and entailed a media campaign that cost between $7 and $10 million.[52]

Janet Champ recalled the day EMI's master tape of the Beatles' recording arrived at the agency in Portland, Oregon:

> We had the master tape right in our hands of the song and we got to put it on and hear all the mistakes and you know [reverent pause] the actual master right out of the vault from Abbey Road and they played it on separate little speakers so you could hear when Ringo dropped the drumstick or somebody made a mistake and it was so beautiful and clear. And everybody in the recording studio came in, came out of the halls all the way down to this room to hear this for the first time. That was a great moment.[53]

The Text

There are three versions of Nike's "Revolution", two hard-rock versions and a softer version with doo-wops. The hard-rock version that attracted attention was a very jerky black-and-white, hand-held camera film, with a few archival inserts, that shows

Nike athletes (including John McEnroe) and ordinary people clowning around while participating in a variety of sports. There are whites, blacks, men, women, and a toddler (who was in fact a cousin of the agency account supervisor). A woman plays "air guitar" and a huge, laughing crowd runs, *en masse*, into the ocean. As Scott Bedbury later recounted, the most striking image was the toddler "running with his arms raised out in front of him, legs turning as fast as they could to keep pace with his upper body. His torso was tipping forward as only a toddler's can, when discovering what it's like to run full out for the first time ... These images", he continued, "were not merely evocative and beautiful, but meaningful, particularly in juxtaposition to each other. The message behind this medley of images marked a new outlook for Nike: the Nike brand now spoke to old as well as young, to women as well as men, to world-famous champions and obscure street athletes, using different images but the same voice."[54] The advert can be interpreted as presenting a theme of empowerment and transcendence and a personal philosophy of everyday life.

The song itself is an allusion to this philosophy, but the harsh rocking sound coupled with wacky, upbeat images adds a level of irony. The clip from "Revolution" includes the opening guitar barrage and the closing yelps of "Alright", but only a few lyrics: "You say you want a revolution, well, you know, we all want to change the world ... But if you talk about destruction, don't you know that you can count me out." That's it. There are four product shots, all so quick they are nearly subliminal. "Nike Air" and the swoosh flash at beginning and end. A few seconds in is a Nike neon sign with swoosh. There is no voiceover, no "Just Do It" (that line had not yet been coined), and only a quick flash of Michael Jordan.

The softer version is in colour, backlit like *Flashdance*, and shows only women. It seems likely that this use of "Revolution 1" indicated a belief that this rendition was "more feminine", rather than "more political", and was intended to deal with women consumers in a way that clearly separated them from the men. It probably aired in daytime to avoid making Nike look "pink" to males—a fear that haunted their management.[55] There is one nanosecond product shot and the "Nike Air" swoosh appears only at the end. The lyrics are the same as the hard-rock version, except the soft version says "you can count me out (in)". There is no voiceover, no slogan, and no Jordan.

A third version uses the hard-rock soundtrack with colour shots of pre-teens playing sports in Nike clothes. The visuals are either saturated with colour or bleached out and show decayed urban settings (chain-link fences, asphalt, graffiti): all this was typical of 1980s MTV, especially of Michael Jackson and Madonna. A logo flashes, but no slogan, no Jordan.

By the time the ad was ready to launch, the stakes were high for Nike. As Phil Knight later recounted,

> The Visible Air launch was a critical moment for a couple of reasons. Until then, we really didn't know if we could be a big company and still have people work closely together. Visible Air was a hugely complex product whose components were made in three different countries, and nobody knew if it would come together. Production, marketing, and sales were all fighting with each other, and we were using TV advertising for the first time. There was tension all the way around. We launched the product with the Revolution campaign, using the Beatles song. We wanted to communicate not just a radical departure in shoes but a revolution in the way Americans felt about fitness, exercise, and wellness.[56]

The Response

Nike credits the "Revolution" spots for its 1987 turnaround, as do historians.[57] Orders increased 30% immediately and sales doubled over the next two years. Historian Walter LaFeber offers that "Revolution" was the moment Nike "found how the transnational corporations could sell goods in vast overseas markets even in the many lands where English was not spoken."[58]

It was also a victory for Weiden+Kennedy. Not only did Nike drastically increase their advertising budget behind the new campaign, a Nike spokesman actually told the trade press, "I guess we're admitting that maybe traditional [television] advertising works".[59] *Advertising Age's* powerful critic, Barbara Lippert, wrote:

> The spot comes from Hipness Central, the New Age advertising capital of the world: Portland, Oregon ad agency Wieden and Kennedy. ... These Nike spots ... offer another example of what's fast becoming the uniform signal of coolness in commercial film: very quick, beautifully edited, tinted black-and-white cuts – some out of focus and jumpy – shot with a hand-held Super 8 camera. This subsection of commercials is quietly redefining TV advertising. There's no announcer, and there's no direct message. We see a discreet logo twice in the beginning and once at the end.[60]

Lee Clow remarked that, with the "Revolution" spots, Wieden+Kennedy had "proved worthy of the Chiat/Day past", and therefore "passed the baton", expanding the elite circle of the Bernbach school to include this small agency in the Northwest.[61] The advert's theme of empowerment and transcendence as a personal philosophy of everyday life formed the basis of multiple advertisements that Wieden+Kennedy were to produce for Nike, and therefore the ad may be understood as foundational to Nike's brand image – one of the most popular and dominant images in the history of branding.

In another *troc*, the producers gained recognition. *Film Commentator* saw Grief and Kagan's ad as finally realising the "commercial-as-art form idea". The review compared Nike's "Revolution" to *A Hard Day's Night*, also a black-and-white film with a home-movie feel. Arguing that the film sold and fetishised the Beatles as "perhaps the greatest purveyors of Western culture since Shakespeare", it concludes:

> We screamed at the magnitude of this in 1964 and calmly live with its consequences today … Grief and Kagan's "Revolution" fulfills the omen of *A Hard Day's Night*: that Pop euphoria and commerce would mix. It's a shorter Beatles promo, but it carries the conclusion and triumph of the Beatles' influence on modern culture.[62]

Nike's main competitor also took notice. When he saw "Revolution" from his den in Massachusetts, Reebok's Paul Fireman concluded that this commercial "was the one that mattered. It was obvious to Fireman that with the new Air campaign, Nike had reevaluated and refocused. Now, in this volatile industry, the tables had turned."[63] Fireman's response was to hire himself a hot creative shop – Chiat/Day.

Yet, in the midst of the positive response, there was also considerable criticism from the media. *Time* magazine said of John Lennon: "Mark David Chapman killed him. But it took a couple of record execs, one sneaker company and a soul brother to turn him into a jingle writer".[64] The *Chicago Tribune* described the ad as "when rock idealism met cold-eyed greed." The *New Republic* commented "The song had a meaning that Nike is destroying".[65]

Exactly what meaning Nike was destroying in the song presented an interesting puzzle. Marshall Blonsky, a professor of semiotics at the New School for Social Research, opined in a vague way that "Music is replete with the meaning of the time. Beatles music has to do with revolt, but the fitness game isn't revolutionary, it's conformism. The commercial's an attempt by advertisers to appropriate the missing past".[66] The meaning the music actually had at the time, however, appears to have been lost – many wanted to give "Revolution" a "missing past" it never had. Chris Morris, the *LA Reader*'s rock critic, asserted: "When 'Revolution' came out in 1968 I was getting teargassed in the streets of Madison. That song is part of the sound track of my political life. It bugs the hell out of me that it has been turned into a shoe ad".[67] John Doig, a creative director at Ogilvy & Mather, remembered anti-Vietnam demonstrations with "bloody police truncheons coming down and Revolution playing in the background. What that song is saying is a damned sight more important than flogging running shoes".[68] *Time* insisted Lennon held to a faith in the "spiritual power of rock", a claim that stood in interesting contrast to Lennon's admission he would have been "crooked" in order to be a millionaire.[69] In the final stab of his attack, Jay Cocks at *Time* reached for the limit: "There are some people for whom rock is not just a diversion or a vocation, or even just a personal expression. It is a lifeline."[70] Rock/pop had come a long way from spoon, moon, June–and "Revolution" had apparently morphed for many listeners from "petty bourgeois cry of fear" to leftist anthem, all catalysed by a sneaker spot.

In this reaction from the press, experts from the academy were consistently interviewed–with their opinions then projected onto "Beatles fans" or even "people" in general, leaving no room for any but an anointed few to claim the music. "People are fed up with the way TV ads are colonising the recent past," Jon Wiener, a history professor at the University of California at Irvine was quoted as saying. "Beatles fans are outraged,"[71] he asserted in another article. The admakers tried to defend themselves by claiming their own right to be "Beatles fans". Kelley Stoutt, an executive at W+K, is quoted in *Time*'s blast: "We're baby boomers, too. This is our music."[72] The implication seemed to have been that, even if you saw yourself as a leftist poet, as a folk artist, as longhaired flower children, or as mavericks in athletics–as these makers did–you had no right to claim fandom (or even cultural citizenship) if you were also an advertiser. Apparently, even Yoko Ono had lost the race for an authentic claim on

"Revolution". Suddenly, it seemed, only the cadre had the right to "hum the tunes".

Some outraged fans did indeed write to Nike to register their disapproval. John Deeth from Wisconsin wrote: "Popular music is, in a sense, our cultural heritage, and I for one am tired of seeing it debased." Deeth remembers that the words to the song were "debated in great detail at the time of its release in 1968", but he nevertheless argues: "I am certain that no interpretation of the song could lead one to conclude that it was written to sell Nike shoes." He then opines that Lennon would not have approved and asks whether they consulted Yoko Ono. Nike's advertising manager, Cindy Hale, wrote back to Deeth: "The music of the Beatles is important to us at Nike, too. ... As Beatles fans and as advertisers, it is not our intention to misguide the public concerning Lennon's original meaning; nor do I think we have done so." She tells Deeth about the process of the permissions – though she does not mention Ono – and says that the use of unusual film techniques and the omission of hard-sell features from the campaign were intended to show respect to the music. She offers the personal opinion that commercial licensing allows young people to hear music to which they would not otherwise be exposed.[73]

The letters kept coming, but most did not focus on radical politics. Instead, they simply claimed the song was debased by commercial use. Jennifer Thomas from Texas wrote, "I believe that using this song only belittles the composition. It is insulting that this meaningful tune is being used in a mere commercial." Kathryn Biggs, who sent with her letter a shredded Nike ad and "the box cover from the last pair of Nike sneakers I will ever buy", was offended by Nike's using "the goodwill generated by the Beatles' song 'Revolution' – the good memories and feelings evoked by it". Bradford Trebach wrote, "I find it very offensive that your company would try to subject this song as a selling device." Meanwhile, as reproduced in this book's epigraph, a Mr Mileski commented: "Your only motive is to make more money for your greedy selves, and in the process you seemingly could not care less that you have trampled and befouled the precious memories of millions and millions of people throughout the entire world. Your kind makes me puke; you low, vacuous, malodorous perverts."[74]

In contrast, Susan Nims, "Beatle Fan", wrote: "In regards to your NIKE commercials I find them very enjoyable and I for one am happy to see the Beatles on television and cannot understand why some people think they are beyond commercialism. The Beatles, after all, were always commercial and it's not like they don't get paid for it! I enjoy your commercials, keep up the good work." Sales alone suggest that Ms Nims' response was the more typical of "Beatle fans" everywhere. For children, the effect seems to have been a generation removed: a seventh-grade student wrote to say, "My class has recently been studying advertising techniques. Your commercial for Nike shoes is great! Putting the song, 'Revolution', in your commercial brings back memories for my parents."[75]

As with the original songs, there were also some outlier comments. Nike reported a "couple of disgruntled responses from people who just don't like rock 'n' roll music".[76] Two letters protested a short clip of a man in shorts. One wrote:

I am writing to you to let you know of a problem with your new commercial. I am concerned with one part. A man in shorts with something draped around his neck falls down to ground. The man does not have any underwear on and is exposed. I am sure that this is an over site [sic] on your part but, something needs to be changed. Thank you for your prompt attention.[77]

Unlike Jean Kilbourne or the makers of *The Ad and The Id*, neither of these consumers accused the advertiser of pornography. Both were offended, but assumed that Nike had simply overlooked the exposure – and therefore probably did not intend to be obscene.

We infer that many, perhaps most, consumers responded positively to the ads, though there was an outcry in the press, often supported by academics claiming to speak for the public, and especially for "Beatles fans". Here, we can hear echoes of voices of those, such as E.D. Hirsch, who pushed back against such assumptions through intentionality theory:

> The myth of public consensus has been decisive in gaining wide acceptance for the doctrine that the author's intention is irrelevant to what the text says. ... But if this public meaning exists, why is it that we, who are the public, disagree? Is there one group of us that constitutes the true public, while the rest are heretics and outsiders?[78]

Perhaps the most significant response was the $15 million lawsuit filed by Apple Records against Nike, Weiden+Kennedy, and Capital Records in an attempt to halt the airing of the commercial. The suit was "a warning to advertisers and the record company: If you think you can use the Beatles recordings to ... peddle anything from bras to beer, you're going to be sued."[79] Apple claimed that, even though Nike had legally obtained permission for the rights to the music, it had used the Beatles' "persona and good will" without permission.[80] This charge is peculiar, given how the ad producers had understood that the Beatles themselves had apparently approved the spot. The explanation perhaps lies in the sequence of unsuccessful suits Apple Records had filed against Capitol/EMI, through which the Beatles' company had attempted to regain control over royalties derived from new formats such as CDs. As Nike's lawyer put it: "What Nike using the music did was afford another opportunity to instigate a lawsuit. And 'Apple is suing Capitol for the third time' generates no headlines. 'The Beatles suing Nike' generated a lot of headlines."[81]

In any case, despite the clear understanding of Nike and Weiden+Kennedy staff that the surviving Beatles had approved the ad, Apple were now insisting that no such approval existed. Writing decades later, Rupert Perry, who had worked at various levels of senior management for EMI and Capitol Records claimed:

> [U]nfortunately neither Capitol nor Ono had bothered to ask Apple, the company which represented The Beatles and their business interests, which Ono was obliged to do under the terms of the Apple board which required the unanimous agreement of all directors. The company's opposition to the project would, in normal circumstances, have been enough to persuade Capitol to withhold the original recording.[82]

George Harrison went on record stating:

> Every Beatles song ever recorded is going to be advertising women's underwear.[83] We've got to put a stop to it in order to set a precedent. Otherwise it's going to be a free-for-all. It's one thing when you're dead, but we're still around! They don't have any respect for the fact that we wrote and recorded those songs, and it was our lives.[84]

By contrast, Paul McCartney, speaking in 1988, was more ambivalent: "The most difficult question is whether you should use songs for commercials. I haven't made up my mind. Generally, I don't like it, particularly with the Beatles stuff. When twenty years have passed maybe we'll move into the realm where it's okay to do it."[85]

The lawsuit is particularly strange because Apple claimed that any Apple action, such as giving consent to a license, required the agreement of the three Beatles survivors and Yoko Ono. Logically, then, Yoko Ono too must have participated in the lawsuit, despite having given explicit permission and public approval. Perhaps for this reason, Bob O'Neill, general counsel and vice president of Capitol-EMI, called the suit "absurd and nonsensical".[86] Reportedly, the action was settled confidentially and out of court after the advertisement had run its course. Later, Nike used "Instant Karma", a solo song by John Lennon, in an advertisement, perhaps reflecting its better relationship with Yoko Ono, while Apple, EMI and Capitol agreed that no Beatles version of any Lennon and McCartney song would ever be used again to sell products.[87] Truly, the Nike "Revolution" ad was a one-off.

Meantime, the lawsuit was news. Phil Knight issued a statement:

> Apple Records is using this groundless suit against NIKE as nothing but a publicity stunt, which makes it appear that NIKE is the bad guy. I'm here to set the record straight. We are not bad guys. We have not used anything for which we have not received permission. ... We, at NIKE, have nothing but the utmost respect for the Beatles and their music.[88]

Fuelling the publicity, Nike took out newspaper advertisements in Chicago, Los Angeles, New York, Portland, and in USA Today describing Apple's lawsuit as a publicity stunt.[89] Accordingly, the story grew and grew and, as Scott Bedbury, who became Nike's advertising director later recalled,

> the surprise... was the way in which nearly every network news show in the country, and many overseas, ran the spot in full to illustrate their stories on the controversy – giving us a priceless amount of free advertising time. Countless magazines featured a news story on the lawsuit, and newspapers reported it on their front pages. After being the beneficiary of this windfall of unpaid publicity for a few weeks, Knight found that being sued by the Beatles didn't feel bad at all, especially since he knew Nike had not acted improperly. If anything, the company's brush with the Beatles only seemed to reinforce its hard-won image as part jock, part rebel.[90]

The Brand

The advertisement seems to have had the impact of transforming Nike from a company that sold shoes into a marketing organisation. Having traditionally operated as a specialist company whose expertise in athletics and close relationships with athletes drove their product design and popularity, they now found themselves successfully competing in a market for shoes as a fashion good or an accessory in which the organising principles were less grounded in function and more in identity and communication-specific consumer market segments. The transformation is best described by Phil Knight:

> For years, we thought of ourselves as a production-oriented company, meaning we put all our emphasis on designing and manufacturing the product. But now we understand that the most important thing we do is market the product. We've come around to saying that Nike is a marketing company, and that the product is our most important marketing tool. What I mean is marketing knits the whole organisation together. The design elements and functional characteristics of the product itself are just part of the overall marketing process. We used to think that everything started in the lab. Now we realise that everything spins off the consumer. And while technology is still important, the consumer has to lead innovation. We have to innovate for a specific reason, and that reason comes from the market.[91]

Nike found themselves not only reorientated, but also at the global vanguard of new ways of conducting marketing. As the sociologists Robert Goldman and Stephen Papson described it: "Nike and its advertising agency, Wieden+Kennedy, currently stand out as leaders in what might be described as a cultural economy of images."[92] This is to say that Nike's primary business concern had transformed into maintaining brand visibility, and this rendered its mission of selling shoes secondary. The ad's theme of empowerment and transcendence as a personal philosophy of everyday life, and its aura of authenticity, formed the basis of Nike's advertising that Wieden+Kennedy produced for them for at least the following decade. In some cases, they sought songs similar to "Revolution", such as the use of "Instant Karma" by John Lennon in an ad in 1992, the use of "The Revolution Will Not Be Televised" by Gill-Scott Heron in 1995, and Andre 3000's cover of the Beatles' "All Together Now" for an ad in 2010. Goldman and Papson describe the successive generation of adverts:

> Wieden+Kennedy has cobbled together a style that sometimes ventures into the waters of political provocation; a style situated at the intersection between public and private discourses where themes of authenticity and personal morality converge with the cynical and nihilistic sensibility that colours contemporary public exchanges. Ranging from moral indictment to showers of praise, Nike ad campaigns have sometimes provoked intense public interest. Within the realm of popular culture, Nike ads constantly surprise and excite, because they are unafraid of being controversial. This willingness to take chances in its ads has translated into Nike's dominance in the sign economy.[93]

The sheer scale of Nike's domination within the supposed "sign economy" that followed is almost staggering to behold. By 1991, Nike held twenty-nine percent of the global athletic shoe market and its sales had exceeded $3 billion.[94] The Nike swoosh became as recognisable at a global level as the Coca-Cola logo, and the enormous sales turned Nike into a blue-chip stock. Many books and articles since written about the rise of Nike mark "Revolution" as the "sea change in the character of the company", the moment when they became "the brash, iconoclastic rebel-turned-near-monopolistic-market-giant".[95]

However, though sales from the "Revolution" campaign were strong, the negative response from some, especially in the media and the academy, appears to have festered, contributing to a focus on Nike that ultimately had longer-term consequences for the corporation and for the brand. By examining Nike's advertising and actions as they unfolded subsequently–that is, teleologically–we can see how this occurred.

Within a year of the "Revolution" campaign, a Nike cross-training ad targeted to women ended with Joanne Ernst telling the camera: "And it would help if you wouldn't eat like a pig." Though Nike executives found these ads very funny, Knight later admitted that many women found them insulting: "They were too hard-edged. We got so many complaints that we spent three or four years trying to understand what motivates women to participate in sports and fitness."[96] Press coverage revealed just how patriarchal Nike was, how the women who worked for and with them were seen as second-class citizens,[97] and the effect was to magnify the perception of a malevolent intentionality behind Nike.

The next year, Nike aired a series with Spike Lee and Michael Jordan–a campaign that won awards and plaudits, but also caused Nike to be accused of manipulating young black kids into buying athletic shoes they couldn't afford. When a boy was murdered, apparently for his Air Jordans, the press exploded with disapproval. In the process, it was revealed to the public that Nike employees were overwhelmingly white, which caused the brand to look racist as well as manipulative.[98] Some fairly creative intentional readings resulted. For instance, a columnist for *US News* said of the campaign's "Just Do It" tagline: "To the middle class it means get in shape, whereas in the ghetto it means, 'Don't have any moral compunction–just go out and do whatever you have to do in your predicament.' There's an immoral message embedded in there."[99] Note that no evidence is offered that poor black people actually read the tagline this way; more to the point, note how the term "embedded" implies that Nike intentionally told urban youth to abandon moral reservation. In this way, blame was attached without evidence of either intention or reader response. In the ensuing fracas, Nike made public service ads, hired minorities, and started community programs. Meanwhile other athletics companies, though also implicated in similar business practices, largely escaped criticism.

The following year, Nike was in trouble for global labour abuses. From there, even as the brand sold across the world, Nike's image accumulated bad associations, aided substantially by work that took Nike as the centrepiece in a political critique. Books like Goldman and Papson's *Nike Culture* and Naomi Klein's *No Logo* were widely reviewed and read. In the end, even the business press was affected. In his *50 Companies that Changed the World*, Howard Rothman listed Nike, but noted its dubious status:

> But just as surely as it had defined the parameters of this sporty but stylish revolution, Nike was singled out for both manipulating it and running it into the ground. The firm drew passionate criticism – sometimes well deserved, sometimes arbitrary – for exploiting foreign workers, raising brand consciousness to an art form, driving prices to outrageous levels, inundating the airwaves (not to mention the sidelines) with its "swoosh" logo, even taking advantage of the millionaire athletes who participated in its omnipresent promotions.

Thus, Rothman observes, "Nike disappeared from the 'in' lists ... it doesn't rule the world right now."[100]

We are not saying that Nike did not commit labour abuses, whether globally or locally, nor are we seeking to defend Nike or elicit sympathy on their behalf. We *are* saying that, dating from the "Revolution" campaign, Nike became a target: big enough, salient enough, and, importantly, suspect enough, to draw fire across a range of issues. The long-term impact of using Lennon's song was thus to attract attention from an audience poised for broad-scale critique. Even Nike's 1990s women's campaign, a feminist-inspired advertisement authored by Janet Champ,[101] couldn't save Nike from becoming the Darth Vader of globalisation.

The long-term effect on Wieden+Kennedy could not have been more different.

The Significance

Through the 1990s, W+K racked up all the top awards for creativity in advertising; their worst criticisms were the jealous howls from disenfranchised USP (unique selling proposition) adherents on Madison Avenue.[102] By 2004, *Inc.*'s "25 Most Fascinating Entrepreneurs" listed not Phil Knight, but Dan Wieden. Each gets a word that summarises their uniqueness; Weiden's word is "independence." His profile opens with a typifying quote: "Being independent provides the freedom to do what you feel is right and that includes the freedom to tell a difficult client to screw off."[103] Now W+K had $875 million in billings. Their clients included Coca-Cola, America Online, Miller Brewing, Subaru, ESPN, Avon, and Nike. *Inc.* lavishes praise:

> W+K ads broke new ground by injecting advertising with irreverent humor, sophisticated film techniques, and hip cultural references. The firm put Lou Reed in a Honda commercial, caused a genuine sensation by using the Beatles' "Revolution" as an insurrectionist version of a jingle for Nike, and then introduced, also for Nike, a cinematic, storytelling approach that helped turn Spike Lee, Bo Jackson, and Michael Jordan into pop icons.[104]

Similarly, *Adweek*, decades later, declared that "Weiden & Kennedy exploded onto the national scene in 1987 with a spot featuring the Beatles' 'Revolution', a controversial move to introduce Nike's Air technology that showcased their bravery, creativity and ability to push advertising into the realm of art".[105]

Other observers echo the same praise – and point to W+K's artistic ethic as the source of their success. James Twitchell, citing Nike's Air Jordan campaign as one of *Twenty Ads that Shook the*

World, remarks on W+K's management style, "which has taken the 'us against them' style of post-Bernbach advertising to a new level. They behave like artists, or at least the Hollywood version of artists. Stomping out in disgust is not just a sign of integrity, it's a way of doing business."[106] The *Inc.* feature's author observes that Wieden+Kennedy has endured by nurturing their creative people artistically, and bringing in local artists-in-residence, "so that the agency's staffers can draw inspiration from close contact with the arts".[107] Large agencies, including J. Walter Thompson ("the aircraft carrier of Madison Avenue"), raided W+K to keep themselves fresh and up-to-date. W+K alumnis thus went out into the mainstream business, evangelising for the arts approach and retraining blue-chip clients.[108]

The difference between the outcome for client and agency stems from their different intentional relationship to the text. Nike was condemned by consumers and the press, who seldom know or notice the agency behind a campaign. Among those who knew or cared that Wieden+Kennedy was behind the spots, it would have been understood that the agency's intention was to make art, even if within commercial constraints. Using art to sell can get you in trouble, because many feel that commerce dirties the sacred – but an allusion to another aesthetic text is a feature through which to confer beauty, complexity, sophistication upon artworks. So, Nike's intention to "use art", and W+K's intention to "make art", had entirely different consequences.

Nike's "Revolution" changed the advertising genre's future choices by breaking what was once the strongest taboo in music licensing – the use of a Beatles' song. Using rock songs for commercials, instead of writing and recording jingles, began in the 1980s and became the norm, eventually pushing studios and composers specialising in jingles out of business. Many other songs, including those with a political subtext, have now been licensed for ads with considerably less hurrah (for example the Who's "Won't Be Fooled Again" was licensed for a Nissan ad). A senior editor at *Rolling Stone* remarked of commercial licensing in 2002: "If it's a good riff, people are going to listen to it … It doesn't particularly bother me or steal the song's meaning from me. I know a lot of people do feel that way, but that's become an outdated way of thinking."[109] Thus, much as Chiat/Day's Olympic billboards changed the *troc* for outdoor advertising, W+K's contribution forever changed the choices of music for the advertising *troc*. However, given that one consequence of the advertisement was that Capitol, EMI, and Apple decided to never license an original Beatles recording again, Weiden+Kennedy retain the aura of having accomplished one of the grand coups of advertising history. Janet Champ, whose idea it originally was to use the song (and who was promoted to copywriter a month after generating the idea) perhaps put it most strongly: "What's more expensive than the Beatles? It was like saying 'we'd like to do a commercial with god.'"[110]

Nike was only one of several quintessential 1980s campaigns that substantially advanced the *troc* by borrowing more extensively from the arts than had been done in the past and refraining from the heavy-handed product features and brand identification that the market research-oriented paradigm of the 1950s had dictated. These campaigns often used literary allusions (as in "1984"), irony (Spike and Mike), wordplay (Altoids), visual tropes (Bennetton and Absolut), musical metaphors (Levi's 501) and even parodies of the 1950s paradigm (Energiser Bunny). Thus, we began to see formal devices revered in poetry, drama, or painting. Yet these canonical cases, as with Volkswagen and other touchstones of an earlier era, sacrificed neither sales nor awareness for creativity. Through this accomplishment, the 1980s advertising leadership extended the influence of the Creative Revolution of the 1960s, increasing their stature as a form even while raising their perceived value among clients.

Five years later, in discussing the contribution of Wieden+Kennedy to Nike's business model, Phil Knight suddenly exclaimed, "Lots of people say Nike is successful because our ad agency is so good, but isn't it funny that the agency had been around for 20 years and nobody had ever heard of it?"[111] Whether this is a fair comment or not, it is nonetheless a reminder that Nike's "Revolution" ad can only be understood by looking at how the various different actors together orchestrated one of the most impactful advertisements of all time.

Conclusion

Both the "Revolution" songs and the "Revolution" ads emerged from an abrupt shift in the *troc* for their particular genre – music on the one hand, and advertising on the other – a move from blatant commercialism toward art. Both times, the genre was becoming eclectic, ironic, parodic, and highly allusory, but also political. Both the ads and the songs were produced by a collaboration of commercial authors – and before it was over, both the Beatles and Nike could "sell anything with their name on it". Both were criticised for the high prices of their products. Yet both groups saw themselves as rebels or artists, and neither identified with business suits. In both cases, the texts were moving in the direction of the *troc*, even to the edge of the horizon of expectations, and thus predictably provoked ridicule, offense, and confusion in some quarters, as well as applause in others. In both cases, however, the offense was related more to a breach of the normal boundaries of commerce than to the constraints of form. In 1968, pop largely remained apolitical, and where it was taken seriously as political discourse, namely in the underground media, it was only permitted to be such if the message was sufficiently radical. By 1987, many felt that the Beatles' music, a hyper-commercial form in its time, had become sacred; so the Nike commercial produced a similar schism, between those who still saw the Beatles as a commercial band and enjoyed having their influence celebrated and those who were strongly invested in the post-Beatles Lennon myth and felt the commercial defiled his memory. Thus, each text produced broadly bimodal responses that could be explained by the perceived authorial intentionality of John Lennon toward both politics and commerce.

This analysis raises questions about the role of memory, attitude, and involvement in the response to an advertisement. The memory that determined the response was not product-related; it was tied to deep-rooted historical, political, cultural, and musical memories. These memories were indeed highly emotionally charged, but some people's memories were the polar opposites of others – and in many cases, memories had substantially changed over time. Therefore, we could not assume that a well-loved song would automatically transfer to a positive attitude, as reported, for instance, for *The Big Chill*. Furthermore, these complex, contentious memories were the result of focused, repeated listening and interpretation at the first moment of the release of the "Revolution" songs. So, the question of involvement was not a matter of manipulating the present audience setting, but of an intense past experience. The heavy intertextuality and crossover of references – to other Beatles' songs, but also to music videos, fashion, films, and the like – undermines any notion that the main cognitive action is manifest in the hard form of the text. This would be true even for children, since the video referred to a contemporary set of MTV signs, while the sound was clearly seen, even by a twelve-year-old, to refer to the songs of a previous generation. The idea that the relevant information is in the commercial's words is also questionable – many were actively misreading the lyrics. Furthermore, the response to the music must be situated within a rapidly changing environment in which the appearance of loved songs in commercial settings would soon go from jarring to commonplace. This dynamic suggests that such responses are tied to a larger cultural context and an ongoing process of practical listening.

For interpretive work, we encourage attention to intention as a way of grounding the potential polysemy of texts and of organising variation among interpretive communities. We encourage critical literature on advertising and marketing (such as those that follow Judith Williamson's seminal text), to engage questions of intentionality in order to avoid dehumanising or mystifying the makers of these texts. Similarly, we seek to draw attention to the problem of how extreme outlier readings become considered as more correct than actual reader responses. Finally, we want to challenge studies that unreflexively render broad social judgements without attention to either actual intention or response. We offer this short book as an example of what an historical poetics could be for advertising—no less critical of corporate wrongdoing, but more firmly grounded in the complexity of creation as well as the multivocality of response. Since both history and poetics are at stake, we strongly encourage renewed development of an approach in which politics and culture are entwined.

The book began by casting doubt on the analytical use of identifying a coherent agent named "the advertiser" whose intentions can be reduced to a singular goal—to sell stuff. What is elementary, but worth repeating, is how advertising agencies, as cultural intermediaries, tend to disappear from the public discourse surrounding who makes advertisements, for what purpose, and in terms of how and why advertisements work as they do. Hence the "Revolution" ad is discussed as purely an output of Nike, which ignores the diverse intentions of the ad's actual producers: the advertising agency and assorted outsourced collaborators. By distinctly organising cultural texts as occupying either the category of the commercial or the cultural, the ways in which these categories blend into one another is obscured. Yet, arguably it is this very dialectical tension between the two that fuels the potency of the ad's affective capacity. Moreover, once we firmly ground the advertisement in the specifics of its production and its reception, it becomes more difficult to maintain prevalent assumptions about singular intentions behind advertisements. We say that there has been a broad failure to take the particular character of advertising production as a rich cultural form in its own right seriously, generating flawed critical analyses. For example, the identification of Nike as a corporate "bad apple", despite their shared practices with much of their competitors, might itself be regarded as a non-systemic analysis of capitalism's own tendencies.

Defendants of the "bad apple" mode of analysis, that is, the mode of specifically targeting a prominent exemplar within a commercial field for critical analysis, will insist that targeting high-visibility corporations is pragmatic because it helps to generate a shared politics of recognition. The attachment of broad critiques to specific corporations means that the bigger corporations become, the more culturally vulnerable they become to critique, which is a form of counterbalancing power. Finally, abstract terms such as globalisation and neoliberalism can be made far more accessible to a broader audience by grounding them in specific critiques of well-known organisations and commodities, thereby reminding people that their own household objects can be directly implicated in news stories concerning corporate abuse and sweatshop labour. From this perspective, targeting exemplar giant brands for extra critical attention, while at one level necessarily arbitrary, is nonetheless no more than pragmatic organisational politics.

That said, there is a strong argument to suggest that Nike requires extra critical attention because it is emblematic of a particular type of brand-oriented organisation and therefore a harbinger, capable of warning us of certain tendencies within capitalism. As Goldman and Papson note, Nike is best thought of as a hollowed corporation whose advertising and branding success have allowed it to disperse its typical business functions, so that what started as a company committed to producing superior running shoes for athletes eventually ends up as a business primarily circulating images and sign values as the source of its value; a business model in which, perhaps, there is no significant advantage to be gained over the competition from the actual manufacture of the product. As Slavoj Žižek tells us,

Nike, because it "not only outsources its material production, the distribution of its products, and its marketing strategy and publicity campaigns, but also the design work itself to some selected top designer agency, and on top of all that, borrows money from a bank", is *nothing*: "nothing *but* the pure brand mark 'Nike', the 'empty' Master-Signifier which connotes the cultural experience pertaining to a certain 'life-style'."[1] To that end, we might argue that it is the very triumph of brand over product that ought to be correlated with the poor pay conditions of the producers of Nike's products; in other words, it is precisely because the added value happens at the symbolic level that those who work at the material level find their labour devalued. If this is the case, then it is precisely correct for Nike to draw more critical attention than their competitors, even in cases when the shoes are made in the same factories by the same labourers, because it is Nike's orientation that intensifies these labour conditions and shapes the practices of their competitors.

However, the problem also concerns what advertising is understood to be and how we are to make sense of it. For example, if the aim is to critique the practice of advertising, then a form of critique that seems to completely ignore the intentions and actual labour process of the advertising agencies seems misplaced. If advertising practice is not systematically analysed, then the risk is that the practice becomes mystified. On this very point we note a tendency within critical thought to imagine marketers to be supreme hidden manipulators, who, behind curtains, are able to control the social order because they have their finger on the cultural pulse and can understand our own desires better than we do. From this position, commodities can be read as deliberately and nefariously encoded with toxic ideology that produce distinctions of race, gender, class, etc.

In presuming the figure of the advertiser to be the Svengali-esque hidden persuader, advertising attracts a level of criticism that is banal and prone to fantasy, but also a criticism that perversely benefits advertisers because they are understood as adding mysterious value to the production process. This is not to say that our consumer culture does not contain ideology and that issues relating to gender representation in advertising are not deeply problematic (obviously they are), nor that advertising is not an ideological process (it certainly is), but it is to say that a thin line separates a contempt for advertisers as hidden manipulators from a reverence for advertisers as the people-in-the-know who drive value. To treat advertising seriously, as a matter of cultural politics, entails paying far more attention to the actual process of production itself and to understand the meaning generated in advertising as not solely primed by this process of production, nor as existing as a stable text to be interpreted by a single person, but instead as something more volatile that emerges in the chaos of the social, often with unexpected and contradictory consequences. Put simply, if we are to have a proper critical theory of advertising, as we must, then we need to dispense with fantasies of marketers as suspicious lurkers in the shadows of consumer culture, who know precisely how to encode ideology into this culture.

We call attention to a continued tendency to imagine advertising as a science. By contrast, some of the most respected professionals in the business have, over the past forty years, come to see themselves unequivocally as artists – and they actively mistrust any attempt to codify what they do into a predictable formula. Imagined "advertisers" who care only about profits and have only product features in mind when creating an ad are quickly becoming an anachronism. In a world where even global giants resist thinking of themselves as, in the words of Lee Clow, "a bunch a guys shufflin' around in suits, you know, with a bunch of strategy documents, because that's bullshit",[2] marketing practitioners are inappropriately cast as followers of a Unique Selling Proposition approach – at which point we end up with an understanding of advertising that is totally disconnected from, and irrelevant to, the profession. In sum, if we are to be practical and relevant, as well as rigorous, engaged, and critical, we need to bring our understanding of advertising and its makers into closer alignment with reality.

We can recognise the moment of the Nike "Revolution" ad as having concretised the popularity of the everyday wearing of sports shoes. Writing these words thirty years later in a university library, it is striking to note that the majority of students have come to study wearing shoes designed for professional sports activities. The fact that this apparently strikes nobody as even slightly odd speaks to how we are still living in the legacy of these extraordinary marketing campaigns and market transformations. Indeed, the possibility that so many people are wearing these shoes because John Lennon, meditating in Rishikesh, decided to address the politics of 1968, reminds us that the collision of culture and politics in the medium of advertising creates the most unpredictable outcomes imaginable.

Notes

Introduction

1   John J. Miller (2006), "Rockin' the Right: The 50 greatest conservative rock songs". *National Review*. www.nationalreview.com/article/217737/rockin-right-john-j-miller

2   Bruce Springsteen (2017), *Born to Run*. London: Simon & Schuster, p. 314.

3   Staff Writer (2016), "1987: Nike Air Spot Features Revolution by the Beatles". *The Drum*. www.thedrum.com/news/2016/05/12/marketing-moment-46-1987-nike-air-spot-features-revolution-beatles-0

4   Staff Writer (2011), "Celebrating Game Changing Commercial Direction". *Directors Guild of America*. www.dga.org/Events/2011/08-august-2011/Celebrating-Commercial-Direction.aspx

5   Nick Ripatrazone (2017), "Story behind Nike's controversial 1987 'Revolution' Commercial". *Rolling Stone*. www.rollingstone.com/sports/30-years/after-nikes-revolution-beatles-commercial-w468218

6   Adam Arvidsson (2006), *Brands: Meaning and Value in Media Culture*. London: Routledge, p. 3.

7   This follows the call made in Arjun Appadurai (1988), *The Social Life of Things: Commodities in Cultural Perspective*. Cambridge: Cambridge University Press.

8   We here reframe a set of questions originally posed by Scott Lash and Celia Lury—see Scott Lash and Celia Lury (2007), *Global Culture Industry: The Mediation of Things*. London: Polity.

Chapter One: Intentionality

1   For example, see Chris Hackley and A.J. Kover (2007),
    "The trouble with creatives: negotiating creative
    identity in advertising agencies". *International Journal of
    Advertising*, 26(1), pp. 63–78.

2   Demetrios Vakratsas and Tim Ambler (1999), "How
    Advertising Works: What Do We Really Know?" *Journal
    of Marketing*, 63 (January), pp. 26–43.

3   Steven Fox (1997 [1984]), *The Mirror-Makers*. Urbana:
    University of Illinois Press, p. 197.

4   W.K. Wimsatt and Monroe Beardsley (1954), "The
    Intentional Fallacy", in *The Verbal Icon*. Lexington:
    University of Kentucky Press, pp. 3–18.

5   E.D. Hirsch (1967), *Validity in Interpretation*. New Haven:
    Yale University Press, p. 3.

6   Judith Williamson (1978), *Decoding Advertisements:
    Ideology and Meaning in Advertising*. London: Marion
    Boyer, pp. 13–14.

7   David Bordwell (1989), "Historical Poetics of Cinema", in
    The Cinematic Text: Methods and Approaches, ed. R. Barton
    Palmer. New York: AMS Press, pp. 369–398.

8   Sut Jhally (1987), *The Codes of Advertising: Fetishism and
    the Political Economy of Meaning in Consumer Society*. New
    York: St. Martin's Press, p. 59.

9   Stuart Hall (1980), "Encoding/Decoding", in *Culture,
    Media, Language*, ed. Stuart Hall et al. London:
    Hutchinson.

10 Bordwell (1989), "Historical Poetics of Cinema".

11 Hirsch (1967), *Validity in Interpretation*, p. 26.

12 Roland Marchand (1985), *Advertising the American Dream:
    Making Way for Modernity, 1920-1940*. Berkeley: University
    of California Press.

13 Michael Baxandall (1985), *Patterns of Intention: On the
    Historical Explanation of Pictures*. Princeton: Yale University
    Press, p. 47.

14 Ibid, pp. 41–2.

15 Hans R. Jauss and Elizabeth Benzinger (1970), "Literary History as a Challenge to Literary Theory". *New Literary History*, 2(1), Autumn, pp. 7–37.

16 J.B. Strasser and Laurie Becklund (1993), *Swoosh: The Unauthorized Story of Nike and the Men Who Played There*. New York: Harper Business.

17 Robert Goldman and Stephen Papson (1998), *Nike Culture: The Sign of the Swoosh*. London: Sage.

18 Jann S. Wenner (2001), *Lennon Remembers*. London: Verso.

19 David Leaf, dir. (2006), *The U.S. Versus John Lennon*. Paramount.

Chapter Two: The Song

1 Wenner (2000), *Lennon Remembers*, p. 110.

2 Colin Campbell and Allan Murphy (1980), *Things We Said Today: The Complete Lyrics and a Concordance to the Beatles' Songs, 1962–1970*. Ypsilanti, Michigan: Pierian Press, p. xxiv.

3 For an excellent discussion on this point, see Campbell and Murphy (1980), *Things We Said Today*.

4 Chris Welch (1968a), "Yes, They Do Grow on You". *Melody Maker*, August 31, p. 17.

5 Bob Dawbarn (1968a), "MM Exclusive". *Melody Maker*, September 14, p. 5.

6 Bob Dawbarn (1968b), "Pop Today and Tomorrow". *Melody Maker*, October 19, pp. 14–15.

7 Chris Welch (1968b), "Oh, What? Own up! Just Groove!" *Melody Maker*, September 21, p. 5.

8 Bob Dawbarn (1968a), "MM Exclusive", p. 5.

9 Chris Welch (1968a), "Yes, They Do Grow on You", p. 17.

10 Bob Dawbarn (1968), "Entertainment has Become a Dirty Word". *Melody Maker*, October 12, pp. 16–17.

11   Tony Mendel (1968), Letter in "Mailbag". *Melody Maker*, November 16, p. 28.

12   Melody Maker cover (1968), "Beatles to Play Live Concert?" *Melody Maker*, September 14.

13   Michael Smith (1968), "Beatles Return to Their Roots". *Melody Maker*, November 30, np.

14   Barry Miles (2002 [1998]), *The Beatles: A Diary*. London: Omnibus Press, p. 278.

15   David Quantick (2002), *Revolution: The Making of the Beatles' White Album*. Chicago: A Cappella.

16   For examples, see Philip Norman (1981), *Shout: The True Story of the Beatles*. London: Pan Macmillan, p. 338; Ray Coleman (1984), *Lennon: The Definitive Biography*. London: Pan Macmillan, p. 562; and Jon Wiener (1985), *Come Together: John Lennon in His Time*. New York: Faber and Faber, p. 246.

17   The Beatles (2003), *Anthology*. London: EMI.

18   Quantick (2002), *Revolution*.

19   John Platoff (2005), "John Lennon, 'Revolution,' and the Politics of Musical Reception," *Journal of Musicology*, 22(2), pp. 241–267.

20   Todd Van Luling (2015), "Exclusive New Video Sheds Light on John Lennon's 'Revolution'", *Huffington Post*, September 11. www.huffingtonpost.com/entry/beatles-revolution-video_us_5640cef2e4b0307f2cae2d69

21   Wenner, Jann S. (1971), "Lennon Remembers, Part Two", *Rolling Stone*, February 4.

22   Campbell and Murphy (1980), *Things We Said Today*, p. xxxi.

23   Miles (2002), *The Beatles: A Diary*, p. 193.

24   Norman (1981), *Shout*, p. 329.

25   Ibid, p. 328.

26   Stefan Granados (2002), *Those Were the Days*. London: Cherry Red Books.

27   See Keith Emerson (1968), "Blind Date". *Melody Maker*,
      August 31, p. 12; Melody Maker, "The Verdict is Yours"
      (1968). *Melody Maker*, September 7, p. 5; Welch (1968a),
      "Yes, They Do Grow on You", p. 17.

28   Platoff (2005), "John Lennon, 'Revolution,' and the
      Politics of Musical Reception".

29   Paul Jones (1968), "Hey Jude/Revolution". *Record Mirror*,
      p. 8.

30   Record Retailer (1968), "Hey Jude/Revolution". *Record
      Retailer*, p. 11.

31   Pete Brady (1968), "Singles Out the New Singles".
      Melody Maker, September 7, pp. 12–13.

32   Welch (1968a), "Yes, They Do Grow on You", p. 17.

33   Melody Maker (1968), "The Verdict is Yours", p. 5.

34   For example, see Platoff (2005), "John Lennon,
      'Revolution,' and the Politics of Musical Reception".

35   Mark Kurlansky (2005), *1968: The Year That Rocked the
      World*. London: Vintage, p. 198.

36   Life poll (1971), "Change, Yes–Upheaval, No". *Life*,
      January 8, pp. 22–27.

37   Norman (1981), *Shout*, p. 358.

38   Welch (1968), "Yes, They Do Grow on You", p. 17.

39   Miles (2002), *The Beatles: A Diary*, p. 278.

40   Susan Lydon (1968), "Would You Want Your Sister to
      Marry a Beatle?" *Ramparts*, November 30, p. 65.

41   Perry Anderson quoted in Wiener, Jon (1985), *Come
      Together: John Lennon in His Time*. New York: Faber and
      Faber, p. 60.

42   Robert Christgau quoted in Wiener (1985), *Come
      Together*, p. 60.

43   Wiener (1985), *Come Together*, p. 60.

44   Tariq Ali (2005), *Street Fighting Years: An Autobiography of
      the Sixties*. London: Verso, pp. 358–9.

45   Jon Wiener (1991) *Professors, Politics, and Pop*. London:
      Verso, p. 290.

46   Both in Wiener (1985), *Come Together*, p. 62.

47   Gary Allen (1972), "More Subversion Than Meets the Ear", in *The Sounds of Social Change*. Chicago: Rand McNally, pp. 213–21.

48   Quantick (2002), *Revolution*, p. 191.

49   Norman (1981), *Shout*, p. 350.

50   Ibid.

51   David Sheff (1981), *All We Are Saying: The Last Major Interview with John Lennon and Yoko Ono*. New York: Playboy Press, p. 187.

52   Wiener (1985), *Come Together*, p. 61.

53   Norman (1981), *Shout*, p. 338.

54   Hunter Davies (1996 [1968]), *The Beatles*. New York: W.W. Norton, p. 289.

55   Paul Zimmerman (1968), "Inside Beatles". *Time*, December 7, p. 106.

56   Chris Welch (1968c), "We Know We're Conning Them". *Melody Maker*, September 28, p. 12.

57   Ali (2005), *Street Fighting Years*, p. 360.

58   Jeremy Gilbert (2017), "Psychedlic socialism: acid communism, acid Corbynism, the politics of consciousness, the future of the left". *Jeremygilbertwriting*. www.jeremygilbertwriting.wordpress.com/2017/09/05/psychedelic-socialism-acid-communism-acid-corbynism-the-politics-of-consciousness-the-future-of-the-left/

59   Ibid.

60   Terry Eagleton (2016), *Materialisms*. New Haven: Yale University Press, pp. 33–34.

61   See the arguments pursued in Campbell and Murphy (1980), *Things We Said Today*, p. xxxi.

62   John Scannell (2012), *James Brown*. Sheffield: Equinox.

63   Kristin Ross (2002), *May '68 and its Afterlives*. Chicago: University of Chicago Press.

64   Newsweek (1969), "The Peace Anthem". *Newsweek*, December 1, p. 102

65   Ali (2005), *Street Fighting Years*, p. 364.

66   Wenner (2000), *Lennon Remembers*, p. 67.

67   Wiener (1985), *Come Together*.

68   Ray Coleman (1984), *Lennon: The Definitive Biography*. London: Pan Macmillan.

69   Davies (1996 [1968]), *The Beatles*.

70   Sheff (1981), *All We Are Saying*, p. 187.

71   Quantick (2002), *Revolution*, p. 183.

72   Ibid.

73   See Simon Frith and Howard Horne (1987), *Art into Pop*. London: Methuen.

74   Davies (1996 [1968]), *The Beatles*, p. xiv.

75   Ibid.

Chapter Three: The Shoe

1   Gbheron (2001), "Ensemble Acting at Its Best", User Comments, *IMDB*, February.

2   For example, see the analysis of Thriller–Kobena Morcena (1993), "Monster Metaphors", in *Sound & Vision: The Music Video Reader*, eds. Simon Frith, Andrew Goodwin and Lawrence Grossberg. London: Routledge.

3   Jean Kilbourne (1979), *Killing Us Softly*. Cambridge, MA: Cambridge Documentary Films.

4   Bernard McGrane, Harold Boihem, and Jonathan Posell (1992), *The Ad and the Id*. Berkeley: University of California.

5   For example, see Edward McQuarrie, Linda M. Scott, John Sherry, and Melanie Wallendorf (2005), "Roundtable on Advertising as a Cultural Form". *Advertising and Society Review*, 6(4).

6   Lee Clow (1991), Interview, Modern Advertising History Archives, National Museum of American History, Smithsonian Institution, Washington, D.C.

7   Walter LaFeber (2002), *Michael Jordan and the New Global Capitalism*. New York: Norton.

8   Geraldine Willigan (1992), "High Performance
     Marketing: An Interview with Nike's Phil Knight".
     Harvard Business Review. https://hbr.org/1992/07/high-
     performance-marketing-an-interview-with-nikes-phil-
     knight

9   Ibid.

10   Strasser and Becklund (1993), *Swoosh*.

11   LaFeber (2002), *Michael Jordan and the New Global
     Capitalism*, p. 61.

12   Ibid, p. 62.

13   See Strasser and Becklund (1993), *Swoosh*; Philip Knight
     (1990), Interview, Nike Collection, Modern Advertising
     History Archives, National Museum of American History,
     Smithsonian Institution, Washington, D.C.

14   Tom Vanderbilt (1998), *The Sneaker Book*. New York: New
     Press, p. 128. See also Jim Riswold (1992), Interview,
     Nike Collection, Modern Advertising History Archives,
     National Museum of American History, Smithsonian
     Institution, Washington, D.C.

15   Knight (1990), Interview, Smithsonian Institution.

16   Clow (1991), Interview, Smithsonian Institution.

17   See Bill Bowerman (1990), Interview, Nike Collection,
     Modern Advertising History Archives, National
     Museum of American History, Smithsonian Institution,
     Washington, D.C. and Strasser and Becklund (1993),
     Swoosh.

18   Strasser and Becklund (1993), *Swoosh*, p. 412.

19   See Steve Jenning (1984), "Industry Sinks Gold in
     Games". *Oregonian*, June 24, D1.

20   See John Jeansonne (1984), "They'll Carry the Torch".
     Newsday, May 5, n.p.

21   Gregg Patton (1984), "These Stars Are Larger Than Life".
     San Bernardino Sun, March 10, p. 79.

22   Mitchell J. Shields (1984), "Breaking the Mold". *Madison
     Avenue*, July, pp. 90–93.

23 Strasser and Becklund (1993), *Swoosh*, p. 413.

24 Clow (1991), Interview, Smithsonian Institution. See Knight (1990), Interview, Smithsonian Institution, and Strasser and Becklund (1993), *Swoosh*.

25 Strasser and Becklund (1993), *Swoosh*, pp. 449, 462 and 472.

26 Willigan (1992), "High Performance Marketing".

27 LaFeber (2002), *Michael Jordan and the New Global Capitalism*.

28 See Knight (1990), Interview, Smithsonian Institution; Dan Wieden (1990), Interview, Nike Collection, Modern Advertising History Archives, National Museum of American History, Smithsonian Institution, Washington, D.C.; and Peter Moore (1990), Interview, Nike Collection, Modern Advertising History Archives, National Museum of American History, Smithsonian Institution, Washington, D.C.

29 Adweek Staff (1999), "Creative: Double Vision – Hall of Famers Dan Wieden and David Kennedy Consider Their Place in Advertising History". *Adweek*. www.adweek. com/brand-marketing/creative-double-vision-39789/

30 Cindy Hale (1985), "12 Months of Advertising or Where Do We Go From Here?" Memo to Peter Moore and Rob Strasser, May 7, Series 1, Subfolder A, Nike Collection.

31 Nike (n.d.), "Why Consolidate to One Agency?" Nike Advertising Strategy Box, Modern Advertising History Archives, National Museum of American History, Washington, D.C.

32 Hale (1985), "12 Months of Advertising".

33 See Wieden (1990), Interview, Smithsonian Institution, and Janet Champ (1992), Interview, Nike Collection, Modern Advertising History Archives, National Museum of American History, Smithsonian Institution, Washington, D.C.

34 Champ (1992), Smithsonian Institution.

35 Ibid.

36 Wieden (1990), Interview, Smithsonian Institution.

37 Scott Bedbury and Stephen Fenichell (2003), *A New Brand World: 8 Principles for Achieving Brand Leadership in the 21st Century*. London: Penguin Books, pp. 31–2.

38 Champ (1992), Interview, Smithsonian Institution.

39 Armond White (1987) "Running on Recall". *Film Commentary*, July/August, pp. 72–5.

40 Ripatrazone (2017), "Story Behind Nike's Controversial 1987 'Revolution' Commercial".

41 Ibid.

42 Nike Staff (1986), "Revolution Meeting". Internal Correspondence, Nike, Modern Advertising History Archives, National Museum of American History, Smithsonian Institution, Washington, D.C.

43 Bedbury and Fenichell (2003), *A New Brand World*, p. 31.

44 Ripatrazone (2017) "Story Behind Nike's Controversial 1987 'Revolution' Commercial".

45 Brian Southall and Rupert Perry (2009), *Northern Songs: The True Story of the Beatles Song Publishing Empire*. Kindle Edition, London: Omnibus Press.

46 Mark Thomashow (1991), Interview, Nike Collection, Modern Advertising History Archives, National Museum of American History, Smithsonian Institution, Washington, D.C.

47 Thomashow, Mark (1986), Memoranda December 19, 22, 23. Nike, Modern Advertising History Archives, National Museum of American History, Smithsonian Institution, Washington, D.C.

48 Champ (1992), Interview, Smithsonian Institution.

49 Jay Cocks (1987), "Wanna Buy a Revolution?" *Time*, May 18, p. 78.

50 Ibid.

51 Thomashow (1991), Interview, Smithsonian Institution.

52 Timothy Taylor (2012), *The Sounds of Capitalism: Advertising, Music and the Conquest of Culture*. Chicago: Chicago University Press.

53 Champ (1992), Interview, Smithsonian Institution.

54 Bedbury and Fenichell (2003), *A New Brand World*, pp. 30–1.

55 Jean Grow and Joyce Wolburg (2006), "Selling Truth: How Nike's Advertising to Women Claimed a Contested Reality". *Advertising and Society Review*, 7(2).

56 Willigan (1992) "High Performance Marketing".

57 See Warren Berger (1990), "They Know Bo". *New York Times Magazine*, November 11, p. 36; and LaFeber (2002), *Michael Jordan and the New Global Capitalism*.

58 LaFeber (2002), *Michael Jordan and the New Global Capitalism*, p. 63.

59 Vanderbilt (1998), *The Sneaker Book*, pp. 125–6.

60 Barbara Lippert (1987), "Roll Over John; the Song Fits, and Nike's Wearing It". *Adweek*, April 6, p. 23.

61 Clow (1991), Interview, Smithsonian Institution.

62 White (1987) "Running on Recall", pp. 72–5. Nike (n.d.), "Why Consolidate to One Agency?" Nike Advertising Strategy Box, Modern Advertising History Archives, National Museum of American History, Washington, D.C.

63 Strasser and Becklund (1993), *Swoosh*, p. 510.

64 Cocks (1987), "Wanna Buy a Revolution?", p. 78.

65 Jon Wiener (1987), "Exploitation and the Revolution". *Advertising Age*, June 29, 18.

66 Cocks (1987), "Wanna Buy a Revolution?", p. 78.

67 Tom Hawthorn (1987), "Turning Pop Classics into Ads Has Rock Fans Singing the Blues". *The Globe and Mail*, July 29, pp. 1–8.

68 Cocks (1987), "Wanna Buy a Revolution?", p. 78.

69 Ibid.

70 Ibid.

71 Hawthorn (1987), "Turning Pop Classics into Ads Has Rock Fans Singing the Blues".

72 Cocks (1987), "Wanna Buy a Revolution?", p. 78.

73 Consumer Letters (1987), Nike Collection, Modern Advertising History Archives, National Museum of American History, Smithsonian Institution, Washington, D.C.

74 Ibid.

75 Ibid.

76 Hawthorn (1987), "Turning Pop Classics into Ads Has Rock Fans Singing the Blues".

77 Consumer Letters (1987), Nike Collection, Smithsonian Institution.

78 Hirsch (1967), *Validity in Interpretation*, p. 13.

79 Hawthorn (1987), "Turning Pop Classics into Ads Has Rock Fans Singing the Blues".

80 Wiener (1987), "Exploitation and the Revolution", p. 18.

81 Hawthorn (1987), "Turning Pop Classics into Ads Has Rock Fans Singing the Blues".

82 Brian Southall and Rupert Perry (2009), *Northern Songs: The True Story of the Beatles Song Publishing Empire*. Kindle Edition, London: Omnibus Press.

83 Interestingly, a fear pervades that a Beatles' song might be used to sell women's underwear. By contrast, Bob Dylan had no such equivalent concern. In 1965, when asked if he would consent to allowing his music to be used in an advert, responded that he would if the product being advertised was lingerie. In 2004 he made good on his comment by not just licensing a song for Victoria's Secret, but also personally appearing in the ad!

84 Southall and Perry (2009), *Northern Songs*.

85 Ibid.

86 Jon Parales (1987), "Nike Calls Beatles Suit Groundless". *The New York Times*. www.nytimes.com/1987/08/05/arts/nike-calls-beatles-suit-groundless.html

87   Southall and Perry (2009), *Northern Songs*.
88   Phil Knight (1987), "Phil Knight's Remarks" Nike
      Collection, Modern Advertising History Archives,
      National Museum of American History, Smithsonian
      Institution, Washington, D.C.
89   Taylor (2012), *The Sounds of Capitalism: Advertising, Music
      and the Conquest of Culture*.
90   Bedbury and Fenichell (2003), *A New Brand World*, p. 31.
91   Willigan (1992), "High Performance Marketing".
92   Goldman and Papson (1998), *Nike Culture*. London: Sage
      Publications, p. 1.
93   Ibid, p. 3.
94   Geraldine (1992), "High Performance Marketing".
95   Goldman and Papson (1998), *Nike Culture*, p. 126; see
      also Berger (1990), "They Know Bo", p. 36; and LaFeber
      (2002), *Michael Jordan and the New Global Capitalism*.
96   Willigan (1992), "High Performance Marketing".
97   Charles Robinson (1990), Interview, Nike Collection,
      Modern Advertising History Archives, National
      Museum of American History, Smithsonian Institution,
      Washington, D.C.
98   Marcy Magiera (1990), "Nike Taps Minority Shop".
      Advertising Age, November 19, p. 18.
99   Berger (1990), "They Know Bo", p. 48.
100   Rothman (2001), *50 Companies that Changed the World*, pp.
      83–4.
101   Grow and Wolburg (2006), "Selling Truth".
102   See Preston Huey (1992), "Agency of the Year? We Need
      More USP". *Advertising Age*, May 11, p. 32.
103   Warren Berger (2004), "America's 25 Most Fascinating
      Entrepreneurs: Dan Wieden". *Inc*, April 21.
104   Ibid.
105   Adweek Staff (1999), "Creative: Double Vision".

106 James Twitchell (2000), *Twenty Ads that Shook the World: The Century's Most Groundbreaking Advertising and How It Changed Us All*. New York: Crown; David Leaf, dir. (2006), *The U.S. Versus John Lennon*.

107 Berger, "America's 25 Most Fascinating Entrepreneurs: Dan Wieden".

108 Danielle Sachs (2006), "Rehab: An Advertising Love Story". *Fast Company*, June, p. 441.

109 Nat Ives (2002), "The Odd Embrace of Marketing and Anti-Establishment Music". *New York Times*, November 6.

110 Rebecca Huval (2015), "Selling Sneakers with Feminist Poetry: An Interview with Janet Champ". *The Toast*. http://the-toast.net/2015/04/27/interview-with-janet-champ/

111 Willigan (1992), "High Performance Marketing".

Conclusion

1 Slavoj Žižek (2011), *Living in the End Times*. London: Verso, p. 210.

2 Clow (1991), Interview, Smithsonian Institution.

Acknowledgements

Special acknowledgement is due to Catherine Coleman who, during her doctoral studies, was instrumental to the archival work that forms the basis of this study. Worth Wagers kindly provided comments and the staff at Repeater have been wonderful to work with throughout; we are grateful to them all: Tariq Goddard, Josh Turner, Miri Davidson, Emma Jacobs, Johnny Bull and Josse Pickard. Finally, Alan Bradshaw wishes to thank Felicity-Jean for being such a good girl when he finished the manuscript.

Repeater Books

is dedicated to the creation of a new reality. The landscape of twenty-first-century arts and letters is faded and inert, riven by fashionable cynicism, egotistical self-reference and a nostalgia for the recent past. Repeater intends to add its voice to those movements that wish to enter history and assert control over its currents, gathering together scattered and isolated voices with those who have already called for an escape from Capitalist Realism. Our desire is to publish in every sphere and genre, combining vigorous dissent and a pragmatic willingness to succeed where messianic abstraction and quiescent co-option have stalled: abstention is not an option: we are alive and we don't agree.